LOVE YOU ALWAYS

BOOKS BY JAN THOMPSON

JANTHOMPSON.COM/BOOKS

CITY/COASTAL/BEACH ROMANCE

Seaside Chapel (7 Books)

JanThompson.com/seaside

Savannah Sweethearts (12 Books)

JanThompson.com/savannah

Vacation Sweethearts (8 Books)

JanThompson.com/vacation

ROMANTIC SUSPENSE/THRILLERS

Protector Sweethearts (6 Books)

JanThompson.com/protector

Defender Sweethearts (6 Books)

JanThompson.com/defender

Binary Hackers (4 Books)

JanThompson.com/binary

LOVE YOU ALWAYS

SAVANNAH SWEETHEARTS
BOOK SEVEN

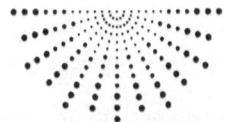

JAN THOMPSON

GEORGIA
PRESS

LOVE YOU ALWAYS (SAVANNAH
SWEETHEARTS BOOK 7)

Published by Georgia Press LLC
Author Website: JanThompson.com
Book List: JanThompson.com/books
Book News: JanThompson.com/newsletter

eBook Cover Design: Georgia Press LLC
Paperback Cover Design: Georgia Press and Deranged Doctor Design

eBook ISBN: 978-1-944188-11-5
Paperback ISBN 978-1-944188-22-1

To my Lord and Savior, Jesus Christ, who died on the cross to save me from my sins and rose again from the grave to give me eternal life in heaven.

∽

For God so loved the world that He gave His only begotten Son, that whoever believes in Him should not perish but have everlasting life.
—John 3:16

READ A FREE NOVEL

YOU ARE READING LOVE YOU ALWAYS

SAVANNAH SWEETHEARTS BOOK 7

Three abandoned children...
Two erstwhile sweethearts...
One missing sister...
And zero problem?

After she kissed him and ran off eleven years ago, Camden never wanted to see her again. But Iris is back in town caring for her nieces and baby nephew, and she needs his help. Can Camden let go of their past history to help Iris with her present crisis for the sake of the children's future well-being?

IRIS'S ISSUES...

When Iris Delaney's five-year-old niece calls her unexpectedly to say that her baby brother has run out of diapers, Iris freaks out and speeds to Savannah to find that her estranged sister, a single mother, has abandoned three kids under the age of six for who knows how long.

Desperate, Iris calls Ming Wei, one of her old friends still living in her hometown, to help her track down the runaway mother. After all, Ming owns Savannah River Investigations, which has been in the news.

To her surprise, Ming sends the last person she ever wants to see again...

CAMDEN'S CALL...

Former FBI agent and burned-out private investigator Camden La Salle is back in Savannah, and is in need of a job. Apparently, stocking grocery store shelves is beyond his pay grade.

Ming Wei has just the right job for him to ease

back into his PI role. Happy to get a paycheck and healthcare, Camden discovers that the client he has to deal with is his ex-girlfriend.

Now he's mad at Ming for setting him up.

At first it's awkward between Camden and Iris, but as things worsen for her two nieces and a baby nephew, the two adults must set aside their differences to keep the children together and try to provide a somewhat normal life for them.

But how can anything be normal anymore for Camden and Iris with their entire past catching up to them?

Love You Always (Savannah Sweethearts Book 7):
JanThompson.com/love

Savannah Sweethearts:
JanThompson.com/sweethearts

For book news, sign up for Jan's mailing list:
JanThompson.com/newsletter

LOVE YOU ALWAYS

CHAPTER ONE

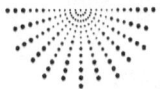

"We're not hungry," five-year-old Peggy said earnestly. "We had turkey and bacon."

Iris Delaney reached for the nearest chair behind her and sat down. The rattan chair creaked, and the armrest was sticky. "Turkey and bacon?"

Her niece nodded. "We shared it with Blue, but he doesn't mind."

"Blue?"

"The cat. He's not really blue," Peggy explained. "He's sort of brown."

The atmosphere swirled around Iris's head. Her heart pounded against her rib cage. "Y-you ate cat food?!"

Peggy shrugged. "Only when we ran out of Cheerios."

"When did you run out?"

"Two days ago, I think."

"Two days! How long has your mother—aargh!"

The scream lodged in Iris's throat.

How could Bianca do this?

How could she leave three kids—five and under —home alone?

Where had she gone?

Iris's head throbbed.

It had been a very long day. She had customer support problems from afternoon until evening at her workplace in Jacksonville. Her shift at the call center wasn't over until eleven o'clock in the evening, but when Peggy had called at nine, Iris's world exploded.

Somehow Iris's older sister, Bianca, had left Iris's number on speed dial on a cell phone in the little girl's possession. Somehow Peggy knew which contact entry said her name.

Auntie Ibis.

When Peggy said that Griffin had run out of diapers and she couldn't stop him from crying, Iris was furious.

A poor, helpless ten-month-old baby running out of diapers? No way.

When Peggy then said she didn't know where her mom was, Iris panicked. She hadn't expected Bianca to pull this sort of trick on her own kids, but she had threatened before to leave them with their fathers—if she could track them down.

Iris hadn't believed she'd carry through with it.

Where are you, Bianca?

Iris had left Savannah years ago and had moved to San Francisco. She had lived there for almost ten years until last year when Bianca had called her, saying that Dad had dementia. It wouldn't be long now before the two sisters lost their dad.

Six months ago, Iris had found a new job in Jacksonville, the closest place to Savannah she wished to be, yet within driving distance of Reidsville, Georgia, where Dad was serving life in prison. That way she could visit him more often in the psychiatric ward, and at the same time, go home far away enough to leave behind a past nightmare she'd rather not relive.

Now, a new crisis had emerged.

Two hours to the end of her shift, and her boss at the call center could not comprehend why she had to leave work and drive up to Savannah to see to the well-being of her two nieces and a baby nephew.

On the spot, Iris quit her job at the call center. She had lasted six months.

Still, she hadn't wanted to work on Wednesday nights, anyway. She would rather go to the midweek service at church, which she had been missing since three people had left the call center in recent months, and she and another worker had been filling in for them until their supervisor could hire new replacements.

She googled and found the phone number of the Savannah-Chatham Metropolitan Police Department. She reported her sister as missing and pleaded for them to send someone to check on the three kids. She had their home address from last year when she had sent them some Christmas presents.

She floored the gas pedal all the way up interstate 95 to Tybee Island, arriving around eleven at night, and having even picked up diapers, coffee, frozen hot dogs, and whole wheat buns at a convenience store on the way. She didn't know how she managed to make that short grocery list, but there it was.

While speeding on the highway in her beat-up old car, she called the SCMPD again, and they confirmed that a patrol officer had been dispatched to the house.

Iris prayed like she had never done before, and somewhere between the exits to St. Simon's Island and Savannah, a couple of high school friends' names popped into her head. She instructed her smartphone to look up some of these names while she drove.

Ming Wei was the first name her phone read

aloud to her. It sounded like he ran a private investigation firm. Perfect! She called him.

Ming didn't mind that she had woken him up. He assured her that she had done the right thing to call 911.

Next thing she knew, it was eleven at night, and she was pulling up on Bianca's driveway between two parked SCMPD patrol cars.

And there they were, her welcoming party.

Two disheveled and sleepy-looking kids standing at the door, flanked by a police officer.

Iris parked her car, took a deep breath, ran up to her greeters, and all was well—

Not!

When she entered her sister's house, she found that the entire interior was in a disarray. It was filthy and grimy and looked like a landfill. The whole place smelled bad.

Iris didn't bother to take off her shoes, and wished she had boots on so she didn't step on what looked like rancid food stuck to the living room carpet.

A couple of windows in the living room were opened to let the outside air ventilate the place, but the horrid stench remained. Iris had never smelled anything like it.

She wondered what Bianca had been doing in this place.

Iris knew that as soon as the officers left, she would have to shut those windows. She was unfamiliar with this neighborhood, and she had three little kids to protect.

Well, right now the kids needed protection from themselves. A five-year-old had run the roost for at least two days, calling all the shots. Somehow they had managed to survive without their mother.

Have they fended for themselves before?

The possibility bothered Iris.

The patrol officer explained that what Iris saw had been how they had found the house. There were no other adults.

Yes, the children had been on their own for who knew how long.

Iris was glad she lived in Jacksonville now. It would have been worse had she still been in San Francisco. The flight alone, considering airport stopovers, would have taken well over seven hours.

Now that she—Bianca's only living relative not incarcerated—had arrived, the patrol officer said they could interview the children. Unfortunately, Peggy and Sibley were too sleepy to talk.

"I put the baby in his crib," Officer Garcia said, holding a ziplock bag containing a disposable phone that Peggy had used to call Iris only a few hours ago.

The other officer had already walked out of the front door.

"Thank you." Iris meant it.

"Detective Zimmerman will call tomorrow morning to follow up. Lock all your doors and windows."

"Is it safe for us to be here?"

"We walked through the house and found no signs of break-ins." Officer Garcia smiled. "Call 911 and we'll be right back."

That's comforting.

Yet Iris knew that only God could keep her and the three kids truly safe.

And Bianca too.

But one thing Iris knew for sure: she wasn't going to sleep tonight.

After the officers had left, Iris was alone with the three lost children of Tybee Island.

She checked on Griffin, who had dutifully fallen asleep again.

And now to feed the older two.

Iris stared at Peggy, who stared back at her with determined eyes, eyes that reminded Iris of...

Mom.

Peggy had her grandmother's eyes.

"Are you sure you're not hungry?" Iris asked again as she realized that she had left the hot dogs and buns somewhere next to Griffin's diapers when she had first arrived. "I can make some hot dogs. Don't you like hot dogs?"

"Only if it's kosher," Peggy said.

"But you're not Jewish."

"Mommy said we try to eat healthy."

"Cat food is not—aargh!"

Peggy stepped toward Iris, who was still sitting down. "Don't worry, Auntie Ibis. Pink likes turkey too."

"Pink? Pink?" Iris began hyperventilating.

Peggy sighed loudly. "Auntie Ibis, stop repeating your questions. I can hear you just fine."

"Tell. Me. Who. Pink. Is."

"A girl cat, of course. She's come to live with us."

"Since when?"

Peggy pointed to a wooden door that had scratches on it. "We found her in the backyard chasing a mouse, but she did it to feed her babies."

"Did you say babies? Baby what?"

Peggy tipped her head to one side, the same way Iris's sister had done. There was so much of Bianca in her daughter.

Where is Bianca?

"Oh, you mean kittens?" Iris widened her eyes. "Baby cats?"

Peggy shook her head. "Everybody knows that kittens are baby cats."

"I know, but...but..."

Peggy's lips trembled. "Please don't send Pink

away. She only has five babies left. We couldn't find the sixth baby. Sibby thinks the pelicans took it."

Sibley is three. What does a three-year-old know about life and death?

My poor, poor nieces and nephew.

"Pelicans don't eat kittens," Iris said, calming down.

"That's what I said. They prefer seafood." Peggy reached over and patted Iris's arm with her grimy, sticky hands. "See, Auntie Ibis. If you don't repeat your words, we can have a normal conversation."

CHAPTER TWO

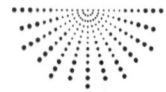

"*A*wkward! I can't see her, Ming." Camden La Salle folded his arms tightly around his chest, his boots tapping fiercely on the carpeted floor of his friend's office.

The Savannah morning sun shone through the wall of office windows, casting a spotlight on his face. He felt blindsided.

How could Ming do this?

"I didn't come home to this," Camden protested.

"This what? You need a job. I have an assignment. It pays well." Ming smiled.

Is that a knowing smile?

Camden frowned. "Of all the clients you have in the world, it has to be her."

"Why not?" Ming eased away from his old office

chair that looked like another find from the local thrift shops.

In fact, the entire office was probably furnished from local secondhand finds, Camden thought, but that wasn't the point of this morning's discourse.

"Why can't you see her?" Ming asked again.

"Um, well, she...um—"

"Vetoed!" Ming laughed.

"Vetoed?" Camden scratched his head. "What?"

"Listen, I was just as surprised to hear from her in the middle of the night," Ming explained. "We haven't spoken in—what?—eleven years? Since you two broke up anyway. Whatever it is, she needs our help now. I'm busy with all these new assignments that Helen is dishing out to me. Besides, Sabine's on bed rest. I have to watch junior until our new baby arrives."

Camden didn't know what to say.

On the one hand, he wanted to help Ming. How could he not? Ming had stood by him through thick and thin. Even when the FBI had fired him for insubordination—whatever!—Ming had not abandoned him.

They went a long way back. All the way to high school.

Same as with her.

Iris had been eighteen, had finished her senior

year at Savannah High, and had started her freshman year at the same college Camden was in.

Camden had graduated from the same high school four years before but had to work for two years to earn enough income to go to college. When he finally made it to his freshman year, he met Iris at their weekly gun club meetings at the student center on campus.

"If you must know, I'm the first guy she kissed," Camden said quietly.

"The only people who didn't know that were Iris's parents."

"Yeah. They didn't like me because I wasn't saved then..."

"We all didn't like you, Cam."

"So there you have it. That's why we broke up her second year in college when she transferred out of state." Camden didn't want to relive it, but it had to be explained to Ming so that he could get out of this assignment.

True, they had only dated for one year, but Camden had always thought they had been serious enough to consider marriage.

"You and I know there's more to it than that. So it has been how many years now, and you're still hung up about her?"

"She'll remember me. Us."

Ming shrugged. "In any case, she's in a bad situation right now. The SCMPD is on it. All I'm asking you to do is organize a community search. Is that too much to ask?"

"There's no way you're putting me on the payroll for that."

"We'll sort that out later. Right now, keep your eyes and ears open. Something's afoot."

"Something's afoot?" Camden had to laugh. "You watching kiddie cartoons with your toddler again?"

Ming shrugged. "Everyone knows there's no way a mother with three young children would just up and leave, you know."

"Right."

"I think the least we can do is to organize the community to help us find Bianca—whatever we can that doesn't get in the way of police investigations. That's our cover story."

Camden groaned. Ming had suspected there was more to Bianca's situation, and now Camden had to do the leg work.

"Besides, you could catch up," Ming said.

"I don't—"

"Iris is alone, stuck with three little kids. She has been away too long. Most of the people she knew no longer live here, except us. I think she knows Tamsyn since we all go way back to Savannah High. Maybe Mrs. Untermeyer. But not anyone else at church. Say, you could invite her to church."

Camden didn't move.

"Don't let your personal beef get in the way of ministry. She needs our help."

"You never forget your first kiss, Ming," Camden finally said.

"Sure you can. I did. When I married Sabine, I forgot and forsook everyone else." Ming swiped his iPhone. "I just forwarded you the transcript of our phone convo. Address and phone number are on there. Keep your emotions out of the interview. Get it done. Get out. As soon as I wrap up this job with Helen—I'm thinking by next Friday—I'll take over, if there's anything to be done. Does that sound good?"

Camden thought about it.

"One week?" he asked.

"Yeah. Get enough info for me to follow up later."

"And you're paying me."

"By the hour, as agreed. In a few months, I should be able to afford to hire a couple more investigators, and then you're free to go wherever you want. If you want to work for me, old friend, you just need to take the assignments I give you. That's how I keep the doors open for business."

Camden drew a deep breath. He needed this

job. He had been out of work for a while, and no law enforcement agency would touch him after that fiasco four years ago. It had been a personal tragedy for him too, didn't they know? Losing his last girl-friend, Daljeet, in that botched operation had been on his mind month after month.

He had taken a hiatus in Ohio—as far away as he could go—for a couple of years, working night shifts, taking part-time security work, and living out of a rented trailer as he tried to hide from the world.

Prayers and constant communication from Diego Flores, his pastor at Riverside Chapel, and Ming Wei, his best friend in all the world apart from Jesus, had pulled him back into reality.

And then two weeks ago, Ming offered him a job at his Savannah River Investigations firm.

Here he was, back in Savannah, ready to start over.

Only he hadn't realized how it could open up old wounds.

And yet...

Camden sighed. He couldn't live off his credit cards. He couldn't sleep on other people's couches and backroom porches anymore. The next stop for him was a cardboard box under a bridge—if he could find an available bridge in Savannah.

He needed this job.

He needed to get back on track.

Swallowing his pride and past hurts, Camden mustered up whatever courage he had lost when Daljeet died, and he buried his face in his calloused hands.

"All right," he bit out. "Sorry about my rant."

Ming came around the desk and placed his hand on Camden's shoulder.

"I will always be your friend, no matter what you say to me," Ming said. "I know what you've been through, and I don't wish to walk in your shoes. I'm sorry that your first assignment at SRI dredges up a past you don't want to revisit."

Camden grunted.

"Unfortunately, if all we end up doing for Iris is organize a community search, I'm not getting paid, though I will still cut a paycheck for you."

"Understood." Camden nodded slowly. "I'll do it off hours if that's the case."

Why on earth did I say that?

"That's the attitude, Cam. Sometimes God works in ways we cannot see, and this could be one of those times." Ming walked back to his chair. "Let's keep it professional, and I'll do my best to get her off your hands as soon as I can. Okay?"

CHAPTER THREE

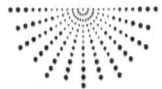

he doorbell rang again at precisely nine o'clock. By then, Iris hadn't slept a wink.

"Someone get the door—oh, that would be me." Iris put down the dishrag on the kitchen counter and picked up her coffee mug.

Before Officer Garcia had left earlier that morning, she had told Iris that a detective would be paying her a visit. Iris hoped they would find Bianca, though somewhere in her heart, she harbored a fear that it could be a pretty useless exercise with Bianca.

She was thirty-seven, an adult with freedom to disappear if she wanted to—child abandonment notwithstanding—and how on earth would they track down one person among the billions of people around the world?

To keep from worrying, Iris had gotten busy after she had put Peggy and Sibley in bed. Fortunately, Griffin had slept through it all.

For the last five hours, she had picked up all the toys, scrubbed gunk off the carpet, thrown out the trash, started the laundry—she should have burned the clothes instead—and vacuumed the floor.

Then she had cleaned up the kitchen, loaded the dishwasher, fed the cats, and wept in the shower.

The doorbell rang again.

"Coming!" The lukewarm coffee sloshed in the chipped mug as Iris made her way to the front door. "Who is it?"

"Savannah River Investigations."

"Oh good." *Maybe Ming's guys can help the police to find Bianca.*

Iris swung the door open and nearly dropped her coffee mug.

Camden La Salle.

"Whoa!" Camden grabbed her coffee mug and righted it in her hand. Their fingers brushed. "Nearly spilled your coffee there."

Iris said nothing. She didn't know what had overcome her when she saw him.

Cam, the only guy I ever truly loved so long ago...

Camden handed her a business card. "This is Ming's card, actually, but he sent me."

"I was expecting someone else. A detective from the SCMPD." It was all Iris could say as she stared at Camden.

He looked older. There was a hint of gray in his hair above his ears.

Still, he looked fit. Muscular.

And he wasn't smiling. "You shouldn't have opened the door so quickly. What if I'm not who I said I am?"

"I should now slam the door in your face?"

"Are we picking up where we left off?" Camden snapped. Then he put up both hands. "I didn't even know you were in town. I only found out a couple of hours ago."

Iris wasn't sure how to respond to that.

"To be fair, I fought against coming to see you. I really did. Ask Ming."

Iris wanted to believe him.

"I'm the new hire at SRI. I do what the boss tells me," Camden said. "SRI cannot take your retainer until the SCMPD is done. Ming and I need to stay out of their way until then."

"So why are you here?"

"I'm here to get some information so we can do a community search."

Iris barely nodded. "I'm not paying you or Ming for that."

"No, no. We want to help."

Iris opened her mouth to speak, but didn't. What was she supposed to say? *I don't need your help, but I do? We've got to find my sister.*

"We're adults. I suppose we can be professional about this," she managed.

"I concur."

"You concur?" Iris almost smiled. "You never used to...ah..."

"Speak like this?" Camden asked. "I've changed more than just my speech, Iris. I'm not the same person you knew eleven years ago."

No! I don't want to revisit the past.

Iris straightened up. "The main business here is to find my sister. She has been missing for at least two days."

"Right."

Iris followed Camden's eyes. She turned.

Peggy was carrying little Griffin in a sling that she had somehow wrapped around her torso, like perhaps she had been taught to do. Behind them, Sibley was sobbing down the stairs with her teddy bear.

"Sibley?" Iris handed her coffee mug to Camden and rushed to the three-year-old. "What's the matter?"

"Want Mommy." Sibley was bawling now.

Iris scooped her up and held her tight. "Shhhh... Mommy will be home soon."

As soon as she said it, she didn't believe it.

Couldn't believe it.

Iris wouldn't put it past Bianca to do crazy things like this, especially when she was high. Otherwise, she could have been a decent mom.

"May I come in?" Camden asked.

"If you're here to help."

"I'm a great helper."

Iris would have to agree. Camden had always been selfless. That much, Iris remembered of him.

"What's that awful smell?" He walked past her.

"That's what I've been asking since last night." Iris followed him, Sibley and the teddy bear heavy in her arms.

"It smells like...hmm..."

"Like what?"

"Not sure, and can't say in front of the kids." Camden placed Iris's mug on the kitchen table and opened the refrigerator.

It was bare save for the hot dogs she had bought the night before.

"First order of things: food." Camden opened the freezer. "Have you fed the children?"

"I tried last night—or early this morning. They didn't want any food. To be fair, an officer was here for over an hour. Too much activity."

Camden lifted up the packet of hot dogs from a refrigerator shelf. "All you got?"

"I picked that up on the way in. I haven't gone to the grocery store."

"Make me a list," Camden said. "I'll go."

"Is Ming okay with that?"

"With what?"

"Doing groceries for us on company time?" Iris asked, shifting Sibley toward her stronger arm. She hadn't carried a child in a while, and her muscles felt stiff.

"This is life support," Camden said.

Iris tried not to laugh. Camden had always put her at ease, and he was doing it again.

Yet he could not possibly succeed. The past would always be there and could not be erased with wit.

Still... "I see you haven't lost your humor."

"I have lost many things though."

He didn't go into details, and Iris didn't want to know. "Let's not go there, Cam."

Nevertheless, Iris felt better with Camden here —the support of an old friend—though she wasn't going to admit it in front of him.

Let's not encourage him.

He seemed to be a stranger to her now.

Eleven years.

Enough time to forget?

She hadn't forgotten how her entire family had felt the shame and shun of the community, when

Dad had killed Mom in a brutally savage way that it had resonated through the southeast beyond Savannah.

Uxoricide, they had called it.

It had driven Bianca to drugs and a string of boyfriends and out-of-wedlock babies.

Three—or more—of them.

The whole tragedy had damaged Iris so emotionally she could not go on with Camden, or anyone else, for that matter.

When she had found out that Camden wasn't sure about his salvation in Jesus Christ, that provided Iris with the reason she needed to end their college romance, which, for all practical purposes, had been chaste because of her family's dating rules.

The problem was, the entire Delaney family, an upstanding Christian family in their old church, had been shamed by one heinous, heartless, horrifying act.

After her father had been sentenced to life without parole, his insanity had cut him off from the entire Delaney family and the church they had attended since Iris was an infant. Since the trial and sentencing, Iris had not gone back to her family's old church, which had since been absorbed by a mega church.

Just as well.

Let the past be buried.

Iris had transferred to a college in San Francisco to finish school and to start over. She had been only nineteen, after all, and had a whole life ahead of her, though bleak it might have seemed at that time.

In her mind, letting Camden go was a penance she had put on herself, but the move had set Camden free from being smeared by the Delaney blight.

While Iris had remained in San Francisco after college, Bianca continued to wander around the country until six or seven years ago. Iris wondered why Bianca had chosen to return to Savannah and Tybee Island—

"Iris?"

He smelled clean. "I do like clean men."

Camden laughed. "I'm glad I showered before I came over, huh?"

"What?"

"You said you liked clean men."

"Why did I say that?" In Iris's arms, Sibley sucked her thumb.

"I don't know. You do look exhausted. When was the last time you slept?"

"Last night—I mean, the night before..."

"What I thought." Camden shook his head. "Before we cart you off to the hospital for exhaustion, you need to get some sleep, Iris."

Someone tugged at Iris's blouse.

"Auntie Ibis, hungry." Peggy looked so pitiful it broke Iris's heart again. "Can we have hot dogs?"

"For breakfast?" Camden asked.

"We also have turkey and bacon." Peggy ran off to the cabinet.

Iris shook her head at Camden, trying to find the words.

Camden knotted his eyebrows together. He seemed amused, more than anything.

Peggy ran back—she couldn't just walk—and lifted two cans for Camden to see.

Iris prayed to God for mercy.

"Cat food?" Camden's eyes darted toward Iris. "You let them eat cat food?"

CHAPTER FOUR

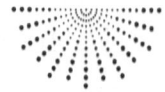

*D*etective Zimmerman from the Savannah-Chatham Metropolitan Police Department looked calm, yet serious throughout the interview with five-year-old Peggy, who had insisted on showing up for the "tea party" dressed up and carrying a yellow purse with smiley stickers all over it. She had also insisted that Officer Garcia, who had shown up for support, and Iris, holding Griffin, sit on both sides of her.

All around them, Blue, Pink, and Pink's kittens walked about like they owned the place.

Iris didn't want to be there. She wanted to go home to Jacksonville, to her hiding hole, to where things were calm and nobody was missing or dead or heading either way.

Still, she was here now, in Savannah, and here

she would remain, for Peggy's sake. For Sibley's sake. For Griffin's sake.

Where are you, Bianca?

And Iris's mother's words popped into her head.

What have you gone and done now, girl?

Iris remained seated on the ratty old couch that oozed cigarette smoke, with Griffin sleeping peacefully against her strained arms, until Peggy's interview was over.

Nearby, on a metal chair with its paint peeling off, Camden seemed to be busy on his iPhone, but Iris was sure he had heard every question that Zimmerman had asked Peggy. Zimmerman had let Camden stay through the visit because he was a friend of the family.

Iris and I have a history. It was a long time ago in college, but we knew each other very well.

Those had been his exact words. Iris tried not to read any finality into the statement, but Camden could be hard to decipher sometimes. Could that have been a question?

"Thank you, Miss Peggy," Zimmerman said, interrupting Iris's mental rabbit trail.

Iris searched Zimmerman's poker face for any signs of frustration. Throughout the twenty-minute interview, Peggy had disclosed nothing, preferring to talk about her smiley purse, dolls, toys, and cats—in random order—with Officer Garcia.

The little girl bounced from one irrelevant thing to another. She was clearly out of focus. It would take more than one day to get information from Peggy about anything.

Poor baby. What did she know? Was it fair for such a young child to know so much?

"You're welcome, Mister Zimmy Man." Peggy slid off the couch. "Sibby! Sibby!"

Her sister appeared from the other side of the couch.

"Let's go, Sibby." Peggy held her sister's hand.

"Where are you going, Peggy?" Iris asked.

"To the pay room."

"Playroom?"

Peggy nodded and pointed to her bedroom. "Pay room in the daytime, Mommy said. Bedroom at night."

"Okay." Iris had more questions to ask, but she was too tired to mouth them.

"When Mommy have friends, Sibby and I go to the pay room and shut the door."

Iris and Camden exchanged glances.

What on earth?

Feeling sick to her stomach was one thing, but a headache that throbbed from the top of her head down to her shoulders now interfered with Iris's concentration on what Zimmerman was saying to her, asking of her.

"Miss Iris, I know you talked to Garcia." Zimmerman swiped his iPad. "I've got some holes here to fill. Tell me about your sister and you. You two are not close."

"Like I told Officer Garcia this morning, we don't talk to each other much, and the last time she called me, it was to tell me that Dad has been diagnosed with dementia. I moved back to the East Coast on account of that."

"Six months ago, right?"

Iris nodded.

Zimmerman had her rehash her job situation in Jacksonville and explain why she hadn't tried to get a job in Savannah.

"I called Bianca at Christmas. Sent the kids some presents," Iris said. "That yellow purse that Peggy likes, for example. It comes with a plastic smiley ring and some bangles."

"This past Christmas?"

"Yes, sir. That's when I found out she had a new baby." Iris glanced at Griffin fast asleep on her lap. He was a cute little baby.

"So you called her on her cell phone?"

"Yes, and she must've saved that number, because Peggy called me yesterday." Iris looked around. "I gave Officer Garcia the phone."

Zimmerman nodded.

"Why are you asking me the same questions?"

Just then, Griffin stirred on Iris's lap and let out a wail. And began to smell bad. "I think I need to change his diaper."

"Like I said, filling holes. No repetition."

"So far."

Griffin cried louder. Iris could barely hear the officer. She stood up. "I'll be right back. I don't live here, but I want my sister found. I hope nothing bad has happened to her."

Zimmerman didn't say anything.

"Would you like to come with me to the baby's room? We can continue to talk there."

And Zimmerman did. "Since you don't live here, there might be a lot you don't know, like whether your sister has a drinking problem or was on drugs."

"I hope not." At the back of Iris's mind, it was bound to recur. "Well, it has been a long time ago, but she promised me she's sober today and not doing anything Mom wouldn't have approved."

"And what wouldn't Mom approve, Miss Delaney?"

"Drinking, taking drugs, cussing, sleeping around, you name it." Iris averted her nose. Griffin's diaper was quite an exhibition.

Zimmerman backed out of the baby's room.

"Unfortunately, my sister has done all of the above many times over—bless her heart."

"Okay. We'll talk more in a minute," Zimmerman said through his pinched nose.

And he disappeared from Iris's sight. She shook her head as she tossed the dirty diaper into the trash can.

Seeing Griffin smiling up at her made her think of Bianca.

What if... No. Banish the thought.

Iris was mad at Bianca.

Sad for the kids.

And terrified of the future.

Lord Jesus, what's going on with my sister?

Griffin looked sleepy, so Iris put him down in his crib. He went to sleep almost immediately.

Iris tiptoed out of the room, leaving a crack in the door so she could hear the baby in case he woke up.

The short and dark hallway led back to the living room, where Peggy was talking to Zimmerman. She was handing him a stack of what looked like photographs.

Iris felt that she had to be in the know if Zimmerman had asked Peggy about something. After all, she was the guardian of these kids now. "What are those?"

"Family photos," Peggy declared. "I'm showing Mister Zimmy Man that Mommy is pretty. Maybe he could hang this everywhere so someone can see it and tell Mommy to come home."

Iris tried not to lose it. Suddenly, a firm arm went around her waist from behind her.

Cam.

Always Camden.

"Let's have a look," Camden said, his voice soft and low, as if to calm Iris. It worked.

Zimmerman lifted the top two photographs in the air.

Iris's face paled. Horror filled her as she blinked away the photos of Bianca stark naked. The photos had been taken in this house, where the children lived.

Zimmerman shuffled through the photographs. "Miss Delaney, do you know what your sister does for a living?"

CHAPTER FIVE

amden listened to the rest of Zimmerman's interview with Iris, but for the most part, there wasn't much Camden could have done, really, whether alone or as a PI with Savannah River Investigations. The SCMPD took missing person cases seriously, especially since a single mother had disappeared, leaving three little kids unsupervised at home.

And those photographs.

No wonder Iris was beside herself.

As soon as she broke down, the interview was over. It could have been over a long while ago, if Camden had had his way, because Iris truly knew nothing. She had no idea where Bianca worked, or whether she owned a car, or how she paid the mortgage for this house, or where she had gotten money for food and utilities.

Sadly, it had been at least two days—if five-year-old Peggy had counted the days correctly—that Bianca Delaney had left without a trace.

Well, to be sure, there would be traces.

And Camden trusted the SCMPD to track down every footprint and fingerprint.

Still, Camden himself had spoken to the neighbors before he rang Iris's doorbell that morning.

The retirees next door could not tell Camden anything. It seemed that Bianca had kept to herself.

The people across the street said they had seen a teenage girl carry the baby to the mailbox and back. That had been a few days ago, and the babysitter hadn't been seen since.

That piece of data, Camden had handed over to Zimmerman to follow up. No doubt they'd try to ask the neighbors to identify the "teenage girl," who could be of any age, really.

Detective Zimmerman seemed like a nice man, rather factual and detailed. Camden had hoped O'Dell had taken the case, but he wasn't available. If it had been O'Dell, whom Camden had known several years ago when he was still an FBI agent— long story—then perhaps Camden could hope to be more informed.

Informed? O'Dell had never been one to speak about his investigations.

Oh well.

Still, a little bit was better than nothing.

Camden had no rapport with Zimmerman. No leverage. No inside track.

As it should be.

After Zimmerman had recorded Iris's statement and had left with those unexpected photographs of Bianca, Camden found Iris cold and shut up in her glass tower. If he didn't know her any better, Camden would say that Iris wanted him to leave.

Was it because he had told Zimmerman that they had a history?

Still, overstaying his welcome would erase any chance he had of ever getting back in Iris's good graces again.

Good what?

He wasn't the one who had left her.

She left me!

Camden had no idea why he felt the need to insulate Iris from some possible truth that she might not want to hear about her sister.

Then again, Bianca could be an innocent victim.

Or the thirty-something-year-old adult might not want to be found.

Camden figured he could dig around a bit

without ruffling Zimmerman's feathers and upsetting the entire SCMPD. At this time in his life, he didn't need a repeat of the fiasco from four years before.

"Thank you for cooking breakfast this morning." Iris ushered Camden to the door. She wasn't carrying either Griffin or Sibley anymore.

"Breakfast? It's almost lunchtime." Camden found himself standing outside the house as Iris stood guard at her castle door, holding an invisible shield in front of her. "Shall we do lunch? I can go pick up something."

"We'll be fine. Thank you. You better get back to work, or you won't get paid."

"I'll work extra tonight to make up for it." Camden figured he could run through the SRI databases to see if there was any new information he could mine.

There was not a single computer in Bianca's house, but surely she had a smartphone better than the disposable one that Peggy had.

And the photographs. Yes, those too.

Camden had snapped a few digital photos of the glossy photographs. He would use image search engines to try to find some leads. Perhaps they would take him to some gentleman's club website or online social activities that Bianca might have been participating in.

And then there was Bianca's history of addiction.

No doubt Zimmerman was already on top of these things.

"Please tell Ming I appreciate his help." Iris's voice was emotionless.

Camden suspected that stripping out emotions —no pun intended—was possibly Iris's coping mechanism. It would be overwhelming to anyone to be left with three kids all of a sudden.

"I'm helping too," Camden said.

"Yes. The community search. I do appreciate your help. I don't seem to know anyone in town anymore—beside you and Ming. Is Tamsyn still living in the area?"

"Yes. She's married now and expecting twins." Camden paused. Then he mustered up his courage and asked Iris anyway. "Would you like to come to my church and meet some new people?"

"I don't plan to be in town longer than I need to. I still have a condo in Jacksonville, and I need to find a new job—uh..."

"What happened?" Camden asked. He could be a patient man. It was a required skill in his line of work. He waited for her to speak.

"I quit my job to come here."

"What did you do?"

"I worked at a customer support call center."

"I thought all that has been outsourced to India."

"Not everything has been outsourced, Cam."

"That's not my point. So you need a job."

"I was an office manager for a number of years until they closed the department store chain a year or so ago. The call center job was all I could get. I don't need much to live on—Why am I telling you all this?"

"Because it's me." *Your Cam.*

Iris's legs moved to one side. Peggy squeezed through the doorway, past the guard. She walked barefoot to Cam.

"Mr. Cam?" Her light-gray eyes blinked in the late-morning sun.

"Yes, Miss Peggy?" Camden was a long way up at six foot three. He squatted down so they could be eye to eye.

"Thank you for feeding Blue and Pink."

Ah, the cats. "You're welcome. They like turkey, don't they?"

"Oh, they love turkey. And salmon."

"Next time I'll bring salmon." Camden glanced at Iris. She bristled.

There might not be a *next time.*

"Do you have cats?" Peggy asked.

"No." How could he? He hadn't settled back into Savannah yet.

Renting Mrs. Untermeyer's basement was only temporary. As soon as he received his first paycheck from Ming, he would find an apartment somewhere. Either that or stay with his older brother and his family for a while.

"Would you like a kitten?" Peggy smiled broadly.

"A kitten?" Camden wondered where the little girl was going with this.

"Yes. A pretty little kitten, Mr. Cam." Peggy raised three fingers. "Five million dollars."

"Peggy!" Iris leaned against the doorframe.

Camden tried to keep his focus on the little girl, not her aunt over there looking pale.

"Well, Miss Peggy, you said five million, but you put up only three fingers. Does that mean I get a discount?"

Peggy shook her head. "I don't want to give you any of my cats, but we need the money."

Need the money?

"Where have you heard such talk?" Surely she was mimicking an adult. Her mom? Camden glanced at Iris.

Iris walked toward them. She leaned toward Peggy. "Peggy, dear, who needs money?"

"Mommy. She says she has to work a lot so we can have money to buy cat food."

Camden kept his voice calm. "What kind of work?"

Peggy shrugged. She rubbed her eyes. "Mr. Cam, do you have five million dollars?"

Camden cleared his throat. He had nothing to his name. "Well, I'm not sure if I can take care of a cat at this time."

"Don't worry. I'll care for the kitten for you."

"So I buy the kitten, and you keep it for me?"

Peggy nodded.

Iris laughed.

"You can bring more cat food tomorrow," Peggy added.

"Tomorrow?" Camden saw that Iris was rolling her eyes, but he didn't know what that meant. "If it's okay with your aunt, I guess."

"You can drop it in the mailbox," Iris replied.

"Oh, that's cold, Iris. You're not inviting me in for tea and cookies?"

"No."

"It's my cat. Have I no visitation rights?"

"It's not your cat until you pay for it. Five million dollars!"

Camden tried not to laugh. "I don't have the money."

"No money, no cat." Iris led Peggy back to the front door.

"Are you pulling my leg?" Camden felt

confused. "You don't make sense. What in the world is wrong with you—uh..."

Iris spun around. "With me? With my family? Is that what you wanted to say, Camden La Salle, Mr. Perfect?"

"Ah, no. Sorry. That came out all wrong. I didn't mean—"

"Didn't mean what? You jumped from cats to my entire family. Are you indicting us all over again?"

"She started it." Camden pointed to Peggy.

"Oh, that's clever, Cam. Blame a little girl. Please leave."

Camden stood still, as though his legs were rooted to the concrete heating up in the Savannah sun. He should have left a while ago and avoided this quarrel.

Iris's shoulders slacked. "All I want to do is take Peggy back into the house, lock the door, and keep the kids safe."

"Only God can keep them safe, Iris."

Iris burst into tears.

CHAPTER SIX

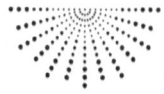

"*T*hat's a no-no, Mr. Cam." Peggy shook her head. "You made Auntie Ibis cry."

Iris wiped her eyes. She didn't want to make a scene. She could tell that Camden looked distressed at the sight of her. "It's okay, Peggy. Let's go inside."

Peggy stood her ground, to Iris's surprise.

The little girl wagged her finger at Camden. "Stop it, Mr. Cam."

"I'm sorry. I didn't mean to make your aunt cry. That's the last thing I want to do her." He looked at Iris. "You do know that."

Yes, I do.

But how could Iris admit it? She would have to eat the humble pie, roll back eleven years, and confess that she had made a grave mistake dumping Camden.

To be fair, they were college kids then. What did they know about life together and marriage? Besides, after what had happened to her God-fearing parents, Iris had lost all faith in the possibility of any wedded bliss.

Best to live life on her own.

Yet now she felt very alone. And helpless. It seemed that the mass confusion in her family, the chaos that followed after, hadn't left the Delaney household in eleven years.

Camden's presence here had brought back all those bad memories—

No.

It wasn't his fault.

It was Bianca's fault. She abandoned her kids!

No.

It wasn't Bianca's fault. She had been as much a victim of her circumstances—

Is it Dad's fault then?

The man was serving a life sentence, paying for his crime.

Iris dared not blame God, but she had come close many times.

"Please tell me, Iris, that you know I never meant to hurt you, not in the past, not now, not ever," Camden said from where he was still standing on the driveway.

"I'm overwhelmed."

"Don't worry about it—I mean, we're concerned, of course," Camden said. "God will help us through. This too shall pass."

Iris nodded. Somehow Camden's voice calmed her down. She wished he'd keep talking, but he was quiet now, waiting for something.

Peggy let go of Iris's hand and stepped forward.

"Are you sorry?" Peggy asked Camden.

"Sorry?" Camden looked surprised.

"You didn't say the word *sorry* to Auntie Ibis, only to me." Peggy clenched her fists and placed them squarely on her little waist. "He made Mommy cry too, and he never said sorry."

Iris gasped. "He? He who?"

Peggy's golden hair shone in the sun. She shrugged. "He came to our house, like others."

"Others?" Iris's heart sank.

Camden cleared his throat. "If I ask the nice detective to come back here, will you tell him about this man who made your mommy cry?"

"What's a tack thief?" Peggy asked.

"He was here earlier. Why didn't you say anything?" Iris added, then figured that Peggy had probably been scared of the stranger in the house, such as Zimmerman was.

Then she realized that she had ignored Peggy's question.

I'm not used to kids!

Peggy looked alarmed. "Will he take away my cats?"

"What do you mean?"

"He said if I tell anyone anything, he will take away my cats."

Iris didn't know how to respond. Her hands shook. In fact, her whole body shook.

"He who?" Camden's eyes were on Peggy, but his hand reached for Iris's shoulder.

Oddly enough, it calmed her down.

Perhaps that was why Camden was here.

"Now, Miss Peggy," Camden said in an even voice. "Our detective friend—from the police department—is a hero. He catches bad guys and puts them in jail. We can trust him."

"A hero? A super duper hero?" Peggy's eyes lit up. "Like you?"

"What? Because I brought cat food, I'm a *super duper hero*?" Camden laughed.

Iris didn't laugh with him. "Cam, just say thank you."

"Thank you, Miss Peggy. I'd be honored to be called a hero, even though I haven't done anything spectacular in my life. In fact, I've done some pretty regrettable things, like letting your aunt go."

"Did she fall?" Peggy asked earnestly.

"Huh?"

"When you let her go, did she fall?"

Camden hung his head.

Iris had to laugh. This had been a rather strange day. She had cried and laughed and cried and laughed. How could life be a seesaw like this?

I need stability, Lord.

Iris stared at Camden. He was on his iPhone.

She heard him talk to Zimmerman. She felt relieved that Camden knew what to do and was taking care of it for them.

Maybe God had indeed brought him back into my life.

For such a time as this.

CHAPTER SEVEN

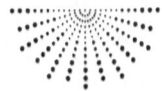

hat afternoon, Detective Zimmerman brought a team of crime scene investigators to Bianca's ramshackle house at the edge of Savannah to comb through the property for latent fingerprints.

In the living room, Camden passed by investigators who continued to take snapshots of paperwork that looked like receipts and bank statements they had somehow found inside the drawer of a table between the living room and the kitchen.

Someone carrying a ziplock bag with a toothbrush in it walked around him. Bianca's toothbrush.

All that activity was based on the photographs a five-year-old had produced.

While it was encouraging to Camden—for Iris's

and the children's sake—that the SCMPD took the case of the missing mother seriously, it was disruptive to the children's afternoon nap, and Camden knew he had to do something about it.

Even if Iris and the kids waited outside the property for the investigators to be done, the entire house could be covered with black fingerprint powder. With Griffin being a crawler and Sibley a curious toddler, Camden was sure it would stress Iris to no end if those two little kids rolled around in the mess.

Zimmerman had a few questions for Iris before everyone who was not from the SCMPD had to leave the house to get out of the way of the investigators.

"I looked through Bianca's bills and such." Iris showed the detective her sister's stuffed desk near the kitchen.

She stepped back, Griffin in her arms. "I didn't know that she was on welfare."

Zimmerman waved to someone, and the person started packing up the paperwork, including the boxes under the table.

Camden stood out of the way. He looked like a pack mule. He had two diaper bags over his shoulders, and in each hand he held the other two kids, Peggy and Sibley.

He heard what Iris had said to the detective.

Bianca was on welfare.

How could she pay for the mortgage of this house? Even the littlest houses in Savannah and on Tybee Island were not cheap.

Camden could ask Ming's wife how much this house would list these days, but he was confident Bianca couldn't make her house payments on welfare checks.

So who paid the rent? The mortgage? Who?

Camden made a mental note to talk to Iris later about doing some sleuthing on their own, such as rummaging through some of Bianca's old bills to find information that perhaps SCMPD hadn't asked for.

Maybe that could keep Iris busy so she wouldn't be stressed about the crisis. Camden knew her well enough to know that she could run if stressed.

The last thing I want Iris to do is run.

"Has anyone cleaned the house?" Zimmerman asked.

"I cleaned a little. I just arrived last night— sometime early morning."

Whoa. Has she just arrived?

"I saved you a box of other documents," Iris said to Zimmerman. "But I didn't see any titles for this house or a car. I don't even know if my sister owns a car."

"We'll get all that information, ma'am. Don't worry about it. We're taking this seriously."

"Thank you, Detective. I appreciate it."

"Where are y'all heading?" Zimmerman asked.

"Mrs. U—I mean, Untermeyer—invited us to stay overnight at her house," Iris said. "Tomorrow, we'll come back here, clean up everything, and get the kids back to their routine."

That seemed to satisfy Zimmerman, and he let Iris go.

Outside the house, her car and Camden's truck were on the side of the road. Camden had moved them before Zimmerman and his entourage arrived.

Somehow, Camden and Iris managed to fit a baby carrier, two five-point car seats, and two crates with five cats in them into those two vehicles.

Camden led the caravan because he knew the streets of Savannah better than Iris, though he had to stop for gas on the way. He appreciated the fact that Iris was as patient as she had always been.

The thing with Iris was not her virtues of patience and kindness. She could be loving and long-suffering if she wanted to, but when things went south, she could scare herself into her shell and refuse to come out.

Eleven years ago when her mother had been murdered, the first thing that Iris did was shut

Camden out, lock the doors, and hide in her closet—so to speak.

It seemed to Camden that God had given him a second chance with Iris.

Maybe.

Mrs. Untermeyer's house was a few blocks away from their old high school. She was sitting in a chair on her porch under a spinning fan when Camden and Iris parked on her cracked driveway surrounded by overgrown weeds. He had promised to mow her lawn for a percentage deduction in his basement apartment rent, and it was time.

But first, the kids and poor Iris.

She was already standing outside the car, hugging Mrs. Untermeyer.

"You look the same, dear girl!" Mrs. Untermeyer exclaimed. "The same!"

"You're as lovely as ever, Mrs. U. Do you remember the cookies you used to make us?" Iris asked.

Nothing had changed, Camden thought as he witnessed the exchange between Iris and Mrs. Untermeyer. It was like a meeting of old friends.

The elderly lady's first name was Rhoda, and she had taught history class in middle school. It was a tough subject, but she made it fun, and the students remembered her long after the school year was over.

Almost everyone whom Camden knew had gone through the rite of passage of being in Mrs. Untermeyer's class, and had stories to tell about her many historical costumes she had worn to class, even though it had been many years ago since Mrs. Untermeyer had to quit her teaching job to take over her husband's business when he died unexpectedly.

She had been known as Mrs. U then, and she was still known as Mrs. U now. Even Mrs. Untermeyer called herself Mrs. U.

And her husband—now deceased—would always be referred to as Mr. U.

"Ah yes. I had Mr. U deliver them to your house —oh, I am so sorry about your missing sister. I've been praying, begging God to return her to her children safely."

"Thank you." Iris turned, but Camden was one step ahead of her because Griffin had started to cry.

Camden tried to unlock the baby carrier and take the whole thing with him, but Griffin wouldn't stop crying.

"Get him out of the seat, I guess?" Camden half asked, half decided. He unlatched the harness.

As soon as he picked up Griffin, the baby stopped crying, and immediately burped something nasty onto Camden's polo shirt.

"Gross! What planet are you from?!" Camden cringed.

The only person who laughed was Mrs. Untermeyer. "Gimme, gimme!"

Her arms outstretched, she *oohed* and *aahed* and made baby noises.

Camden waited for Iris to approve. As soon as she nodded, Camden handed Griffin to Mrs. Untermeyer.

"You are the cutest baby in the world!" Mrs. Untermeyer exclaimed.

Iris walked past Camden to get Peggy and Sibley out of their car seats.

"Where is she taking Giffey?" Peggy asked, alarm in her voice.

"Nowhere. We're all going inside," Iris said. "She has cookies."

"And toys from long ago." Camden chuckled. "Long, long ago. Like another century."

"What's century?"

"A hundred years old."

"A hundred! She's a hundred years old?" Peggy climbed out of the car.

"I didn't say that," Camden protested.

"Watch your words, hon," Iris said as she picked up Sibley, already asleep.

"Whoa, Iris. Did you just call me hon?"

"I don't recall."

"Subconsciously, you wanted to call me *hon*. Funny, you've never called me *hon*, even way back when."

"Then that's your proof."

"But you wanted to. And you did."

When Iris didn't respond, it almost made Camden's day.

CHAPTER EIGHT

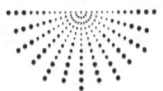

"It's so surreal." Iris spread the bed sheet on a patch of grass beneath a live oak in Mrs. Untermeyer's backyard. She put four little shoes—they belonged to Peggy and Sibley—in each corner so the bed sheet didn't flap up in the late-afternoon wind.

"What's so real?" Peggy asked loudly as she continued to run laps around the trees with Sibley.

"God is real," Camden said. He was nearby, putting a vinyl tablecloth on a wooden picnic table. He placed melamine plates on the tablecloth to hold it down.

Peggy stopped running and came over to Camden.

Iris waited to see what they were going to talk about.

"What is God?" Peggy asked.

"*Who* is God," Camden corrected her. As per his usual gesture, he glanced at Iris.

Iris tried to hide her surprise and sadness and suspicion that her sister hadn't told Peggy about God. Iris was more apt to believe that was the case, because Peggy didn't seem like a kid who would miss anything.

"Who is God?" Peggy repeated. She stood next to the picnic table, her innocent eyes looking upward at the tall Camden.

"God is the creator and maker of the universe," Camden explained.

"What's you nee?" Peggy asked.

"Universe." Camden pointed all around him. "The moon, the stars, the sun, where we live, the air we breathe..."

"Everything?" Eager eyes seemed to absorb the new information.

"Everything. And God made you and me." Camden pointed to Iris. "And lovely Auntie Ibis over there, sitting pretty under the tree, waiting to be...uh..."

Iris ignored him. That was a bit of the past there. Camden had talked like that, always turning a conversation to involve her, to include her, as if to do otherwise would cause the discourse to be incomplete.

"Blue and Pink too?" Peggy asked.

"Yes, cats too."

"Wowee. He must be a big God!"

"Yep." Camden squatted down. "If you want to know more about God, let's go to church this Sunday—if it's okay with your aunt."

Iris nodded. "Of course it's okay, Cam. It's only Thursday, and we just haven't reached the weekend for me to think that far ahead."

"Thank you, Iris. Would you like to visit my church?" Camden asked.

"Not the one we used to attend?"

Camden shook his head. "Sad news about that one. The leadership messed up—immorality and whatnot—and that church split and died a horrible, fiery death."

"Seriously?"

"Well, it broke up and was never heard of again."

"Okay."

Peggy seemed to be oblivious to the side conversation. She tugged at Camden's shirt. "Do we get to play at church?"

"They do have toys in the kids' area, but the most important thing we do at church is to study the Bible, which is God's Word."

"He only says one word?" Peggy's eyes widened.

Iris saw Bianca's blue eyes in her daughter.

Where are you, Bianca?

"God says a lot of words," Camden told Peggy. "All that He has said to us that we have recorded in the Bible is called, collectively, the Word of God."

Peggy didn't seem to understand. She lifted three fingers in the air. "Giffey says *two* words."

Iris watched Camden handle it.

"What words does he say?"

"Da-da." Peggy started running off. "He only says it when he points to you!"

Camden swung toward Iris.

Iris pretended like she didn't hear anything. She got off the bedsheet. "Mrs. U probably needs some help bringing the food out. I'll go see what she needs."

Camden came alongside her. "You said something was surreal earlier."

"Cam." Iris stopped in her tracks. "One of us has to stay with the kids."

"I'll stay. What's surreal?"

"This whole thing with Bianca suddenly being missing. Makes me wonder what kind of trouble she's in, you know."

"I hear you. We can only pray that God would keep her safe. Tomorrow we're mobilizing the community to help us find Bianca. Don't worry, okay?"

Iris nodded, but inside she was worried sick.

What if something bad had happened to Bianca? Who was going to take care of the kids?

Iris had to go back to work—

Oh. Yeah. I quit.

Then it meant she had to find a new job.

"If you know of anyone looking for a data entry person or an office manager position, would you let me know?" Iris asked.

"Sure. Uh, does that mean you're staying in town?"

"I can't live off credit cards, Cam. Once my sister is found and the kids have their mother again, I'm going to leave." Iris had wanted to tell Camden not to get his hopes up, and now she had.

"I understand."

"Do you?"

"I'll come see you in Jacksonville."

"If I let you." Iris laughed, then turned solemn. "I wonder where Bianca is."

"Zimmerman is working hard to find her. O'Dell—you don't know him—told someone who then told me that our good detective had put in overtime."

Iris nodded.

"Maybe you shouldn't go back to the house," Camden said.

"Zimmerman didn't indicate any danger." Iris

reached for Camden's shirt. Then retracted her hands. "Don't worry about us, Cam."

"Until the investigation is over, until Bianca is found, I just don't think it's safe."

"On the word of a five-year-old cat whisperer?" Iris knew that Zimmerman would have to go for stronger evidences than photographs.

Camden frowned. "We don't know what's going on, right? We don't know what happened to Bianca or where she went."

"No mother in her right mind would abandon her kids," Iris said.

"I agree. Still, I don't want to scare you, but I think something bad happened to your sister."

Peggy began to bawl.

It startled Iris. She didn't realize Peggy was listening to their conversation.

What to do now?

Iris had never had kids before.

"Peggy." Camden lifted Peggy up. "Do you remember what I said about God?"

Peggy half nodded. "He's very big."

"Yes. He's a big God, and He can take care of us. Don't worry." He nodded to Iris. "Don't worry, right, Auntie Ibis?"

Iris barely nodded.

"Tell you a verse I memorized when I decided to join the FBI," Camden said.

"What behind?" Peggy asked.

"Never mind. The point is that the Word of God is always true. Several years ago, I was in a tough situation..." Camden's voice started to crack.

Iris wondered what that was about.

"And my friend Ming reminded me what Pastor Flores—you'll meet him Sunday—recited to us from the Bible. Want to hear it?"

Peggy nodded.

"It's from Psalm 56:3," Camden said.

Whenever I am afraid,
I will trust in You.

"That means we trust God no matter when, no matter what," Camden added.

Peggy pointed to Iris. "Auntie Ibis, did you hear that?"

"Good verse," Iris said. "Thanks for the reminder, Cam. You're amazing."

"I know."

CHAPTER NINE

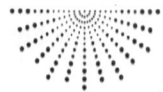

*C*amden woke up in a cold sweat on Friday morning, having dreamed that Iris Delaney had left him a second time and had vanished to parts unknown—just like her older sister.

He blinked, trying to get a bearing of where he was. He heard owls. The night was dark. The air-conditioner kicked in.

Then he remembered.

He was in his brother's guest bedroom, which used to be a girl's bedroom. If he turned on the light, everything would be hot pink, from the four walls to the bedspread to the shower curtain.

However, Camden couldn't complain. If his niece hadn't moved out to a college dorm, he would have to sleep on that uncomfortable couch in the living room downstairs, with his brother's old, snoring bloodhound.

He jumped into a hot shower, put on the same clothes he had worn the day before, and padded downstairs to his brother's kitchen to find that it was only 5:25 a.m. Only his niece's old cat was awake. Barely.

He made a pot of coffee, and sat down at the kitchen table to check his email.

He sent a note to Tamsyn Ruttledge to tell her what was going on with Iris and asked for any connections she might have so they could widen their search. He copied Iris on the email.

As he drank the black coffee, he heard footsteps. They were heavy, and he knew to whom they belonged.

"Morning, Cam." Bryce La Salle headed for the cabinet. "Why are you up so early?"

"Thought I was missing something." Camden chuckled. "Turned out I should have stayed in bed."

"I know the feeling." His fifty-something older brother poured thick coffee into his mug and sat down across from Camden. "I'm glad you're back in town. Ming working you hard?"

"Easing me into a heavy workload." *I think.*

"You're unattached and can go places. What I wouldn't give to be young again and travel the world."

Camden studied his brother. "You can still travel while old."

Bryce nearly spurted coffee out of his mouth.

Camden jerked to one side to evade any possible projectile. "Hey, I just showered."

His brother laughed. "You know, Louisa had been looking at some possible Mediterranean cruises we could go on."

"So go."

"Can't. Someone has to watch the store."

Ah, the River Run Indoor Range. It was a thriving business only because Bryce had worked very hard at it. "Your daughter could keep an eye on things while you're away."

"Are you kidding me? I'm not leaving a gun range to a twenty-year-old college kid. No way."

"How long are you going to be gone?" Camden asked. "If you go, that is."

"Twenty-one nights. Plus a couple of extra days on both ends to fly there and back." Bryce frowned. "Almost a month."

"So you need a manager."

"I need a manager. Someone to watch my pro shop, manage my instructors, and maybe even teach." Bryce slowly looked up. "Want the job?"

"Huh? Me?" Camden finished his coffee even as he was thinking about it. He wondered how to take on one more job if he had planned on spending all his off hours protecting Iris and the kids. "Part time?"

"Full time. It will allow me to semiretire."

"You're too young to retire."

"And you're too old not to have a full-time job."

Bryce was right. On the entire drive from Ohio to Savannah a week ago, Camden had prayed for God's will for his career. He wasn't confident that working for Ming would be forever. At some point in time, he was going to get tired of the same old, same old.

But firearms. He couldn't get tired of handling them, shooting them, teaching others to safely use them. Target practice had always been his therapy.

"Maybe you're onto something."

"I know I am." Bryce refilled his cup. "I've worked too long, too hard to build up my shooting range to let it go to the pits. I trust you. I know you had issues at the bureau, but I'm thinking you're more mature now and you've learned your lesson and all that. And tell me you didn't lose your right to carry."

"Nope. I'm in the clear." Camden took a deep breath. "I take full responsibility for what happened four years ago. Not only did I lose my professional reputation, I also lost the girlfriend I was supposed to marry."

"You haven't lost Iris though. She's back in town, you told me."

"I meant Daljeet, from four years ago." Wasn't he listening?

"That wasn't meant to be then. Did you love Daljeet?"

What kind of a question is that? "We were thrown together by work and spent a lot of time together."

"Not the same thing. You said you were 'supposed to marry' her. That's not nearly the same as *wanted* to marry her."

"Whatever. Daljeet passed away. End of story."

"Yep." Bryce leaned against the kitchen counter. "What's going on with you and Iris?"

"That's the thing. Nothing is going on. She came back Wednesday night. I saw her Thursday. Spent all day with her."

"No spark?"

"I sense a wall between us."

"Walls can come down."

Camden nodded. Then stilled. "However, if this is not God's will, then we'll go our merry way and never see each other again."

"Then pray. That's the best thing we can do. And will you pray about handling my day-to-day operations at the gun range?"

"I will. When do you need to know?"

"ASAP. Louisa already has the cruise dates marked." Bryce pointed to the magnetic calendar on the refrigerator door. "See those red crosses? Twenty-one nights from Athens to Rome and everywhere in between. Last week, Louisa bought a new set of luggage."

"No kidding."

"I think that's a big signal that I'd better take her or else. It is our thirtieth wedding anniversary, after all."

"Wow, Bryce. Thirty years. Congrats. Go. Enjoy yourself. I'll fill in for you." That was all Camden could promise his brother.

Camden wondered what God was doing in his life. He had been in such a drought, a desert for so long, and suddenly he had rolled into an oasis. Jobs were everywhere—jobs that he would want to do—and the only woman in the world he'd ever loved was now right there in front of him...

Just out of reach.

CHAPTER TEN

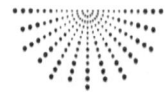

Who could refuse an offer to help clean the house and babysit three young kids? Not Iris.

Before Mrs. Untermeyer could finish her sentence, Iris had jumped for joy.

After breakfast, all five of them—two adults and three happy kids—made their way back to Bianca's house on Tybee Island.

Mrs. Untermeyer didn't want to impose on Iris to have to drive her back to her house on the other side of Savannah, so she drove her own vehicle, a company van emblazoned with the words "Christmastown USA" on the side.

The twice retired businesswoman—and once history teacher extraordinaire—was in talks to sell a majority of her company shares to Melvin Theroux's businessman nephew from Atlanta. Her health was failing, and she didn't want to run Christmastown anymore. Her husband and father-in-law had been instrumental in building the business, but her children didn't want anything to do with it.

The Therouxes themselves, members of Riverside Chapel, were also up there in age, and Melvin Theroux had mentioned wanting to sell his poinsettia nursery to the same nephew, who had to make up his mind about moving to Savannah to take over the business.

Iris wasn't sure why Mrs. Untermeyer had told her all that until they arrived back at Bianca's house with mops, buckets, rags, cleaning detergent, and dust masks—the last item being something Mrs. Untermeyer had around her house because she was allergic to dust. Basically, she had thrown into the back of her van whatever she had.

"You said you were an office manager for some years," Mrs. Untermeyer said.

"Yes, ma'am." Iris nodded as she opened the crates to let the cats out.

The poor cats hadn't done as well as dogs would have, being carted all over the place. The cats would rather be home—thank you very much—and immediately went to their favorite spot: food corner.

"Mr. Theroux would handle the day-to-day

office matters for Christmastown until his nephew is able to move to Savannah, but he's been busy caring for Marie."

Iris wondered what she was getting at, and she didn't want to be presumptuous of opportunities.

Calmly, she poured cat food into the three bowls. The cats meowed and went for the bowls. She refilled the water bowls with fresh tap water and waited.

"I was thinking, if you could send me your résumé, we could take a look and see if you might help us at Christmastown," Mrs. Untermeyer said. "We need someone to sort through our decorating schedules. I'm past retirement age. I can't keep up with our existing clients, let alone schedule new ones."

"Thank you. That's very kind of you. However, I'm not sure if I could work at an office and watch three kids. I don't have the money for babysitting."

"I thought of that." Mrs. Untermeyer put on some gloves. "My eyes aren't so good anymore, and I can't see my computer screen straight. What if I bring my computer here, and you can work out of the house? If they need you at the office, I'll watch the kids, and you can go for a couple of hours."

"Wow. I need to pray about this. But no, I don't need your computer if all your office information is on a cloud."

"A cloud? What's what?"

Oh dear. "I mean, I have my own laptop, and I can get Internet connection."

"Oh, Internet. That, I understand." Mrs. Untermeyer nodded.

"This sounds like something I could do, if it all works out." Iris moved on. "How long do you need an office manager?"

"Unfortunately, when Mr. Theroux's nephew comes to town, he might bring his own people."

"When does he come in?"

"Probably end of August or September."

So it seemed like this could only be a temporary position.

Well, income is income.

"Understood. I'm also praying that the police finds Bianca sooner than that. When she comes home, I'll help her get settled back into life with her kids, but I need to go home."

"Home? To San Francisco?" Mrs. Untermeyer held a mop.

"I lived there for years, but I meant Jacksonville where I live now. I'm starting to know where all the shops are."

"Isn't Savannah your real home?"

Hmm?

"I could never leave this town." The elderly lady

smiled. "I have too many happy days here when Mr. U was alive."

Iris simply nodded.

"That's why I have to keep Christmastown going. We haven't been getting new clients the last two years. It seems that not too many businesses are decorating for Christmas anymore."

"Is it the backlash, maybe, against Christmas?"

"There's that, but I think it's just money. If you can cut expenses and do your own decorating, wouldn't you?"

"I suppose. For me, I just put up a small tabletop Christmas tree, all the trims hot-glued to it."

Mrs. Untermeyer looked horrified. "Girl, that's not Christmas!"

Iris had no idea how they ended up talking about Christmas. It wasn't a season for her to consider in the middle of a crisis. But there was a paying job prospect in the midst of their out-of-place conversation.

Still...

All she was concerned about—no, worried sick about—was her sister's whereabouts. If something awful had happened to Bianca, who was going to take care of these three precious children?

Would it be up to Iris then?

She wasn't ready. No.

She could barely get used to living alone, let alone have a pop-up family.

Lord, the best thing that could happen now is for Bianca to come home.

CHAPTER ELEVEN

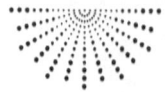

"*Y*ou're not going to believe it, Cam," Iris said excitedly over the phone. "Mrs. U said I could send her my résumé, and she'd consider me for a position at Christmastown. Help her with scheduling and other office work. And she'll let me work from home if it works out. That will save me daycare money."

"We're both having a good day," Camden said. "This morning my brother offered me a job at his gun shop."

"That's cool. But don't you already have a job as a PI?" Iris wiped up the mushy banana from Sibley's high chair tray. She watched as the preschooler smeared the rest of it in her hair.

Preschooler.

Then it hit her.

Shouldn't Sibley be in preschool this fall?

"Yeah, but Bryce wants to take his wife on an anniversary cruise to Europe, and he doesn't trust his college-age daughter to run the gun range. So I'm going to try to juggle both."

Iris sat down beside Sibley at the kitchen table. "He still has that gun range? At the back of his old gun store?"

"Yeah. Same location."

"So, two jobs. That'll keep you busy."

"I told him I need a week to get settled into my PI job for Ming and get this community search organized. And then I'll let him know."

"Don't worry about the search," Iris spoke into the phone. "Pastor Flores gave Jerome Pendegrast my number, and he called this morning. We discussed a few things."

Silence.

"Cam?"

"I want to be in on this."

"We're going to the meeting this evening, right?"

"Yes, but..."

"You're not being excluded, Cam."

"Good. Just checking."

"Jerome wanted to catch up. It has been eleven years since I left Savannah. He wanted to know what's been happening with my life. You know him. He's that kind of guy."

"So when do we catch up?"

We? Iris didn't know how to respond to Camden.

Across the kitchen table, Peggy was sliding off her seat.

"One sec." She waved at Peggy. "Finish your sandwich."

Then Iris was back on the phone. "Cam, I have to go. We're having lunch. Peggy is trying to run away without being excused."

Run away?

Iris wondered if that ran in the family.

❧

By two o'clock in the afternoon, Iris and Mrs. Untermeyer were done. They had deep-cleaned the entire house, top to bottom, but had left Bianca's bedroom untouched. For some reason, Iris had the idea that perhaps Detective Zimmerman might return to find more evidence, but more so, she herself wanted to have a look.

Perhaps she could see something they had all missed.

Yet Zimmerman had told Iris on Thursday that it would take a while for DNA collected to be processed and matched. In fact, he had cautioned her that it could be months—sometimes a year—

before they would know the identities of the people whose DNA were in the house.

It would take less time for fingerprints to be matched, but it wasn't going to be overnight.

All Iris could do now was wait.

And pray.

Black soot and fingerprint powder cleaned out of the furniture, grime and filth scrubbed out of the floors, the house looked ready for show.

Yeah, sure.

Iris had found rotting trims around the windows when she had been scrubbing. Even Mrs. Untermeyer agreed that the whole house needed a new paint job and possibly a new roof, with the telltale signs of water seepage on the ceilings in the kitchen.

Iris opened the refrigerator and retrieved the last can of soda. She jotted down one more thing to get at the grocery store. Her expenses had gone up. She had been tapping into her savings to pay for these needs.

I need a new job pronto.

Iris wondered how Bianca had bought this house, and who was paying for her mortgage while she was on welfare. Bianca had never been one to manage money. She could barely make her apartment rent back in the days when there had been more communication between her and Iris.

Some six or seven years ago.

Somehow, after that, there had been a fall-out between the two sisters, for reasons that Iris still hadn't figured out fully.

Iris relived the embarrassment she had felt on Thursday when she could not answer most of Detective Zimmerman's questions. The questions had been overwhelmingly haphazard, but now that Iris had a day to mull over them, she became curious.

What did Bianca do for a living?

How did she make the car and house payments?

Who were those children's fathers? Did they provide child support?

What kind of trouble was Bianca in? Could it be related to the unsavory photographs that Peggy had shown the detective?

Why had she abandoned her kids?

Iris made her way to the front door to check the locks. The kids were all taking a nap. She yawned but decided she had to stay up. Had to keep watch. Protect these babies.

Mrs. Untermeyer had gone home after promising to be back after dinner to watch the kids while Iris and Camden went to the community search organization meeting. For all practical purposes, Mrs. Untermeyer was now their free babysitter.

Iris chuckled as she remembered overhearing

Peggy call her Grandma U as the little girl helped them to sweep the floor and take out the trash. Mrs. Untermeyer hadn't minded.

Iris sat down with her can of soda at the kitchen table and was about to tether her laptop to her iPhone, when she saw the text from Camden.

Camden.

Always coming back into her life in one way or another.

She knew that Camden would see from his end that she had read the message. She figured that was enough. It was hard to dial back eleven years of lost time. They had moved on in many ways.

She didn't know what Camden wanted from her now, but she had nothing to give him.

Iris's primary objective was to take care of the children until the SCMPD brought her sister home.

Perhaps she could speed up the process by calling on mutual friends. Bianca had been living in Savannah for about five or more years now. Of course, the SCMPD was probably following the same leads.

But some people talked more if they weren't talking to law enforcement.

The first person Iris thought of was Tamsyn Ruttledge nee Pendegrast. She and Iris had been in the same Bible study group at Savannah High, back when it was okay to have Bible clubs at a public school, same as any other student clubs and organizations.

Tamsyn was still living in Savannah, according to Camden, and being a tour guide, she probably knew many people, past and present.

She checked her email and saw that Camden had not forgotten to forward her email to Tamsyn. His postscript reminded Iris that Tamsyn was still on vacation, but Iris sent a note to follow up anyway. She figured Tamsyn could reply whenever she received it.

The bad news was that Bianca didn't have any social media presence.

The good news was that almost all their friends—whom Iris remembered—were online on Facebook and Instagram, including Savannah High alumni.

While she hated to dredge up their past family life, it had been long enough that, perhaps, their family friends—if they were still in town—would be forgiving.

Iris swallowed her pride and tried to friend all her old high school pals, including those who had shunned the Delaney family, and Bianca's old friends. Pretty soon, she had close to four hundred people she sort of, kind of, knew—and never wished to meet in real life.

She posted a cropped photograph of her sister

and added a plea for any information of her where-abouts. It was a difficult note to write.

It finally sank in.

Bianca was not only still missing forty-eight hours after Iris had arrived in town, but she could be dead.

If she had experienced a relapse in her addiction problem—

The next thing Iris knew, she was on hold for Detective Zimmerman.

"I just—just want to ask if you have any news about my sister," Iris said feebly when Zimmerman came on the phone.

"We're doing all we can, checking all the places she might have been, people she might have been in contact with." His voice was calm. "We have a lot more information to go on now, if that helps."

Iris wanted to feel better, but she didn't. "Did the disposable cell phone that Peggy had provide any information?"

"Yes, ma'am. Again, we're doing our best, and as soon as I have some news, I'll let you know."

"Some people from our church—I mean, Cam's church—are putting together a search team."

"Good. Let me know anything you find."

"We will." But Iris knew it didn't work the other way around.

She opened her mouth to say something else,

but a baby scream stopped her. "Oh, I'd better go. Griffin just woke up."

Zimmerman wished her a good afternoon and hung up.

Minutes later, Iris gave Griffin his bottle as she finished dictating to her laptop some decent content to post on social media. She hoped that her old friends from high school and college she had just tried to reconnect with a couple of hours ago would come through.

Pretty soon, Peggy and Sibley also awoke from their afternoon naps, and that was the end of anything else Iris could have done online, as she had to watch the kids, feed them, bathe them, and spend time with them.

Iris wondered how Bianca had any time to work outside the home at all.

CHAPTER TWELVE

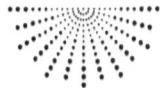

"We can't pick up where we left off, Cam," Iris said when they were alone in the car.

Camden wove through traffic on River Street. "Why not?"

He had thought of that very question in recent days. How would life have been different had he been married to Iris all this time?

"It's been eleven years," Iris said. "We're older now."

"Wiser, they say." Camden pulled into the parking space. The car faced a very old wall, probably nineteenth century.

They would have to walk to Piper's Place, but they had twenty minutes to spare. Camden didn't want Iris to think that he had purposely parked this far so they could have alone time, but she didn't seem to notice.

It wasn't like they had to go back to the children right away.

Mrs. Untermeyer had the kids for the evening while Camden took Iris to meet with Jerome Pendegrast and his friends organizing a community search for Bianca.

Jerome's team had done this before a few years ago when a middle schooler had gone missing. She was found quite quickly and returned safely to the family, and the informal group of mostly retirees from Riverside Chapel had been largely responsible in making the community aware of the missing child.

Still, that had been a child.

Bianca Delaney was in her late thirties, an adult who could go anywhere she wanted.

Abandoning her own children was one thing, but there was no law that said she couldn't cross county or state lines and drive on to parts unknown.

Or worse yet, kill herself.

Camden was careful not to bring that up.

Right now, Iris seemed to be preoccupied with the past. Ironically, if she kept at it, she might not worry too much about her missing sister.

"Life is life, Iris. Sometimes people come back into our lives, sometimes they don't." Camden stepped in his parking brakes. "God does what He does, and we just need to let His perfect will play out."

"Meaning what?" Iris unbuckled her safety belt.

"I have a lot to deal with in my life, and so do you. At this point, for some reason, God brought us both back to Savannah. You know I spent the last four years in Ohio?"

"I didn't. Why did you go there? A job?"

"No." Camden mulled over his thoughts. Wondered how to explain it.

It had been four years since Daljeet was fatally shot in that botched FBI operation. It had been his fault, and his alone, and that fact had eaten him alive.

He had left the FBI amid a sea of accusations and internal investigations that had resulted in a reprimand from his supervisor.

Unable to get a job anywhere, he had wandered to his uncle's house in Ohio. Spent four years stocking shelves in Dayton.

The change of scenery had cleared his mind— and his bank account.

Broke, he had come back to Savannah after Ming offered him a job.

First assignment: babysit Iris and the kids.

"Something on your mind you don't want to talk about?" Iris asked.

"Why aren't you married yet?" Camden asked.

"You're a private investigator. You didn't look me up?"

"No."

"Thanks for respecting my privacy."

Camden nodded. "What's the name of the senator's son you dated out in California after you dumped me back in college?"

Iris bristled. "Why?"

"Just curious."

"That was a long time ago. Old history." Iris looked at him squarely in the face, and Camden knew what was coming. "So are we."

Old history?

He shouldn't have dug up the past. To Camden, eleven years hadn't been that long ago.

Somewhere at the back of his mind, he was hoping against all hope that there might have been a possibility they could rekindle their relationship.

Perhaps it was time to let it go.

"Shall we call a truce, Iris?" Camden pulled the parking brake. "Let's help your sister's kids. Then we go our separate ways."

"Promise?"

Camden wished he could read her mind. "The last time I promised, my fiancée died—oh boy, I didn't want to tell you that."

"She died?" Iris's jaw dropped.

"Work accident." That was all she needed to know.

"I'm sorry. So sorry."

"We had the entire wedding planned. I pulled through. She didn't."

"You worked together?"

Camden nodded. "Don't pity me."

"And don't pity me either, Cam. Someday, your bride will come. I'm not her."

Camden wasn't sure he agreed.

"Eleven years ago, you wanted to marry me because you thought I needed a fresh start from the tragedy in my family. I was only nineteen, Cam. You were what? Twenty-three?"

Camden shrugged.

"I don't think you were thinking straight," Iris continued.

"I was—it wasn't because of—never mind. We need to go. They're waiting for us at Piper's." Camden opened his car door. "Just so you know, I'm doing this community search for you and with you, but I don't want anything in return."

"Fair enough."

"As far as I am concerned, we have nothing more to say to each other, right?"

"Right."

"But could we be friends?" Camden asked. Perhaps Iris might leave a door cracked for him.

"We could, yes."

Still, the way she had said that spoke of a reluctance so great that Camden probably could not bridge the chasm. For all practical purposes, the relationship they had once cherished no longer existed.

"That's all I ask." Camden opened the door for Iris, as he had always done back when they had been an item.

CHAPTER THIRTEEN

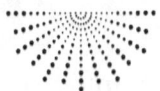

he search party leadership meeting was detailed and organized. The minutia gave Iris a headache, but she went along with the way they conducted the meeting, because if that was what it would take to find her sister, then so be it.

Someone had reserved a private room on the third floor of Piper's Place, that old café that Piper Peyton owned, and the meeting was called to order as soon as Iris and Camden arrived.

"What do we know? What don't we know?" Jerome Pendegrast asked.

Iris remembered Tamsyn's father from way back in high school.

Sitting next to her, awfully close, Camden

leaned over and whispered in her ear, "Tamsyn's baby sister has been missing for over ten years."

"Oh. She's still missing? So sorry." Ah. So that was why this group had been organized.

Quietly, Iris prayed for Jerome, that God would bring his missing younger daughter home safely as well.

"We can't get any information out of SCMPD, as you know," someone responded. "Legal reasons and all that."

Iris didn't recognize the woman.

"However, we fanned out, asked all the neighbors within a three-to-five-mile radius of Bianca's house, and also all the coworkers," someone else said.

"Bianca has had a string of boyfriends. Some worked at the same grocery store as she, and some were shoppers."

Iris's jaw dropped. She almost cringed at the new information these people had found about her sister. She didn't know that Bianca had worked at a grocery store.

Camden raised his hand. "We called as many as we could, but most of them are tight-lipped."

"Why?" Iris asked.

"That's what we want to know," Camden replied. "We can ask around, but Detective

Zimmerman has warned us not to interfere. They're doing all they can."

Jerome checked off another item on his display board. "Next, social media. What's happening?"

"We have connected with Bianca's classmates from high school. No information on college."

"Bianca went to work right after high school," Iris said. "I've friended a bunch of people."

"Everyone who knows someone is on the lookout for her." Jerome looked in Iris's direction. "We will do our best to help the SCMPD find your sister. Don't worry."

Iris wanted to cry.

"We don't know many things," Jerome continued. "We know that the house is in Bianca Delaney's name, but we don't know—yet!—who is paying the mortgage every month. We know that the house is not in foreclosure."

"Someone bought my sister the house?" Iris asked.

Camden shrugged.

"We don't know who fathered her kids—"

Iris raised her hand. "Whoa. Is that necessary information?"

"This is a private meeting. Nothing we discuss here goes out unless we all agree," Jerome said. "However, several of us talked to her coworkers at the grocery store, and they said that Bianca herself had told a few of them that she was getting child support from one of the fathers."

Iris wasn't sure if she should walk out of the meeting.

Camden leaned toward her. "We've already informed Zimmerman, and he said this is helpful."

Iris nodded.

She spent the rest of the meeting stunned.

If she had been overwhelmed since she arrived in Savannah, this took Iris over the edge. She had a splitting headache by the time Jerome adjourned the meeting after having given each leader a quadrant to be in charge of.

But she had to give it to them. If Bianca were still anywhere near Savannah, Iris had no doubt she would be found soon.

Please let her be alive, Lord.

Bianca had to be alive, Iris decided. There was no way Iris could raise her sister's kids all by herself.

I'm not ready.

"For coffee?" Camden asked.

Iris looked up. Had she been mumbling to herself?

"Some of us are going downstairs to have some cake. If you'd like to join them, I'll go. If you want to go home, I won't stay."

Iris started to tell him to do whatever he wanted. Then she realized she needed a ride home. Well, couldn't someone else take her home? Sure, but she didn't know most of these people. She had been gone from Savannah a long time.

As for Jerome, she knew him, but it had turned out that he was living on his riverboat docked not too far from Piper's Place. He could walk home.

"You go right ahead, Cam. I'll call Uber for a ride home," Iris said.

"No."

"Snappy, aren't we?"

"Look, Iris. We don't know what happened to your sister. Heaven forbid she got involved in something nasty. I don't want you abducted on the way home."

"It's only fifteen minutes from here."

"Anything can happen in fifteen minutes. I need to pro—uh..." Camden drew a deep breath. "Let's go."

"How about a compromise? We do coffee for just a little bit, not stay long, then leave."

"All right. Sounds good to me."

When Mrs. Untermeyer returned Iris's text and said all the kids were asleep and they could stay out as long as they wanted—considering it was Friday night—Iris relented and stayed for an extra half an hour.

Camden profusely apologized that it was his

fault for making her wait for his second cup of coffee.

He was still apologizing when they walked back to the car.

Iris stopped him. "Camden, once again, it's okay."

"Is it, really? You didn't look too happy back there."

"Happy? How could I be when my sister is missing? She could be dead. Should I party on Friday nights until she comes home?"

"It wasn't a party. You had no cake."

"I couldn't eat cake. I'm trying to lose some weight here." Iris pinched her own waist.

"Sure. Excuses. But I made you stay, and I'm sorry."

"Stop. How many times do I need to tell you it's okay?"

Camden knotted his eyebrows and leaned toward her. "You sure?"

"You're ridiculous, Cam. You haven't changed in that regard. You're still uncertain about things in life, aren't you?"

"Well, maybe some things."

"Why don't you take it at face value? That's a simple way to handle it. Don't read too much into what I say. When I say it's fine, accept it."

"If you say so." Camden unlocked the car door.

"See, there you go again. If this and if that." Iris stepped toward him. "Let me put it to rest that our coffee time was fine. Truth be told, I enjoyed those thirty extra minutes of not having three little kids running in circles around me—or running me in circles."

"I guess I did some good." Camden held the passenger side door open for Iris.

"Besides, you didn't spike your coffee. I'm happy for you, Cam." She wished she hadn't said that, but there it was. She had noticed it, and now Camden knew she had remembered some things from their past.

Iris sat quietly in the car as Camden pulled out of the parking lot.

When they had merged with traffic, Camden said, "I'm not the same person you knew in college. Two years after you left, I met Jesus and trusted Him as my only Lord and Savior."

Iris didn't interrupt him. If Camden had a need to tell her about his salvation testimony, she felt that it was only polite to let him speak.

"You did me a big favor when you dumped—I mean, left—me. You drove me to God. And I got saved. Ming took me to his church. When that church folded, we went to another church, and that's the church I'm attending now."

At a red light, Camden leaned back. "I've been

growing spiritually since then, but I'm a slow learner sometimes."

"We all need God, Cam. Look at me. I've backslidden in more ways than one."

"You? Backsliding? Say it isn't so."

"Well, that spiritual girl you knew in college? She's gone, Cam, replaced by a humiliated hypocrite who can't even share Christ with anyone now without bringing up a family tragedy."

"It wasn't your fault. You're not your dad. He's not you. He's an adult, making adult decisions."

"He's mentally ill, Cam. He killed...murdered... Mom." Iris wiped her cheeks. "I fear for Bianca, that she might be dead."

"Shhh..." Camden reached for her shoulders. He rubbed them and kept his arm around them, as he drove with his other hand. "We're not going to speculate, right? We trust God to keep Bianca safe."

Iris nodded. "Since when did you become so confident?"

"My confidence is in Christ. It's no longer in myself."

"You know, for years I prayed for you that God would give you confidence." *Might as well admit it.*

"Confidence? You mean, courage? Is that what I need?" Camden laughed.

"God gave you more than what I asked. He gave you salvation in his Son, Jesus Christ."

"Absolutely," Camden said as they drove onto Tybee Island. "I've prayed for you too, Iris, that you'd be more decisive in life."

Decisive?

Why is Cam digging up my past?

Iris was surprised that he had chosen to pray for her regarding something she had been trying to forget for eleven years.

"Is that okay?" Camden asked.

"Okay to pray for me? Sure." Except for decisiveness. Why did he have to pray about that? What was he trying to remind her of?

"Ever since I got saved, I've been praying for you. God is why we're both still here."

Iris unbuckled her safety belt after Camden had parked the car. Mrs. Untermeyer had left the front door light on for them.

Mrs. Untermeyer's car was parked behind Iris's on the driveway.

Across the front of the house, the curtains were drawn. It looked dark inside the house.

"He gave you the grace of salvation, Cam," Iris said as she unlocked the front door.

"And He gave you the mercy of deliverance."

"Mercy and grace."

"Isn't that interesting?" Camden folded his arms across his chest.

Iris nodded. "Almost two peas in a pod."

"I'm not sure what that means."

"We'll figure it out later."

"Together?"

"I don't know about that." It was the best Iris could offer him. Unless, of course, she decided otherwise.

Oh boy, Camden was right. She needed to be more decisive.

Lord, teach me to make wise decisions.

CHAPTER FOURTEEN

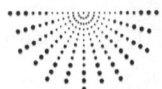

*I*ris had been up since four in the morning because she had forgotten to turn off her laptop and mute her iPhone. The two machines had vied each other all night for the most pings, whistles, buzzes, and general notification noises. Plugged into their chargers, they didn't run out of battery.

Ninety-nine percent of those social media notifications were sympathy notes.

What Iris really wanted were leads to Bianca's whereabouts.

It seemed as though she had simply walked off the face of the earth.

Thanks to the lack of sleep, Saturday was fast becoming the longest day ever in Iris's life, even longer than the day the judge had sentenced Dad to life in prison without parole. Mentally imprisoned in his own mind and physically incarcerated for a crime he couldn't explain, Dad was still languishing in that penitentiary.

For the last eleven years, Iris felt as though she and Bianca had been in prison along with Dad, their lives forever changed by a mentally deranged act that had taken the life of their beloved mother. It had been the strangest thing for Iris to experience.

Until now.

Remaining on the passenger side, Iris closed her eyes in the hot afternoon sun beating down on her through the windshield. The air conditioner was on.

Still, July was often unkind to Savannah, its residents, and tourists. The summer strokes of heat and waves of humidity bristled and prickled Iris day in and day out.

Yet July in the South wasn't the reason she had moved across the country to San Francisco—before reasons pertaining to Dad had persuaded her to return to the East Coast.

Sure, she could have used a new college and new environment as an excuse.

But for the most part, she had wanted a new beginning.

For some reason, she had decided—rightly or wrongly—that her new beginning in a new place, a new space, didn't include Camden La Salle.

There he was—about a hundred feet away from their car parked at the curb—knocking on the hundredth door today, sweating up a storm in his cotton polo and rugged cargo pants. He had worn hiking boots for good measure.

Iris's feet had been awfully tired, and she decided to stay in the car for this leg of the door-to-door project.

Camden was handing out fliers to the neighbors, and the search teams had widened the radius to ten miles because the grocery store that Bianca worked in served a wider community than her neighborhood.

Other search teams and community volunteers were in other zones. Iris reminded herself to send Jerome Pendegrast a thank-you card for his effort in trying to locate Bianca.

Something trickled down her cheek and chin. At first she thought it was sweat, sitting in the air-conditioned car. Seriously, Camden should take the car to the mechanic because the AC wasn't working too well.

Then she realized it wasn't sweat.

She couldn't stop the tears. She just couldn't.

She heard a car door shut.

"Hey, hey, hey. What's going on?" Camden's voice was a mix of alarm and exhaustion.

Iris felt Camden's hand on her left shoulder. She shook it off.

"Let's go pick up the kids," Camden said. He started the car. "The kids would be wondering why we've been gone all day, although we don't know if Griffin is aware of anything, being a baby and all."

"We're not done yet," Iris protested.

"You are. Besides, the girls might be wearing out Mrs. U by now, so this is a rescue mission."

"Ha-ha."

"We'll get the kids, take y'all home to your sister's house, and I'll come back and finish up. I'll join one of the search teams. Don't worry about it."

They were on the road before Iris realized that Camden meant it. "I need to find Bianca. Please."

"Let's pray," Camden said. He didn't hold Iris's hand like they had used to do. "Father God, You know where Bianca is. We need to find her for the sake of the kids. Give us some news, something, so we can take the next step. In Your Son's Name I pray. Amen."

"Amen." Iris wiped her eyes. She had to be strong for the kids.

"See what God has done for us in this time of crisis, Iris?"

"What?"

"He brought Mrs. U to watch the kids so you and I can hand out fliers."

Iris nodded.

"He put Zimmerman on the case. I have confidence in the SCMPD."

Iris tried to detect any unsureness. It wasn't there. "You sincerely believe they will find Bianca?"

"I didn't say that. I said that I am confident the SCMPD will do everything they can to find the missing mother of three little kids. A mother doesn't just walk out on her babies unless something is seriously wrong."

"That's what I'm afraid of, that something has gone wrong and Bianca is dead."

"Don't say that." Camden parked outside Mrs. Untermeyer's house. "Listen, we've told Detective Zimmerman everything we know about Bianca, her history, her contacts. All the information we've gathered in the last two days has been handed over to him. Let the system work."

Iris nodded.

"And wait upon the Lord. The more we fear, the more we have to trust God."

"Right." Still, she broke down again on Mrs. Untermeyer's porch. "I don't want the kids—especially Peggy—to see me like this. I need a minute."

She sat down in one of the two Adirondack rockers on the porch to catch her breath.

Her iPhone pinged incessantly, but she couldn't bring herself to check it.

Oddly, or not, Camden didn't leave. He sat down in an adjacent rocker.

"Are you going to check your phone?" he asked. "Oops. Wrong question."

"You must think I'm weak because I'm afraid to look at my phone to find an email or a message telling me what I don't want to hear."

"No, no. Sometimes it's the unknown that scares us, you know." Camden looked like he wanted to hold her hand, but he clasped his own hands over his knees instead. "We don't know where Bianca is, and that causes us anxiety. We don't know what happened to her, so that's stressful."

"You were in the FBI."

Camden nodded.

"So you saw this sort of life-and-death situation all the time?"

"Well, it depends. Sometimes I work on art theft cases, and those artists have been dead for hundreds of years." Camden chuckled. "Usually no one dies over stolen art, you know."

"In the last big case that...uh...got me fired, we were chasing down an international fugitive. That was a hairy one." Camden didn't say any more.

"Let's not dig up the past."

Camden breathed in deeply. "There is a past we do need to dig up, Iris."

Iris knew that was coming. "Not now, Cam."

Camden nodded. "Well, let's get the kids. You're going to be okay?"

"Yeah. Thanks for sitting with me a minute."

He had always been kind like that.

Iris didn't know now why she had broken up with him. He would have endured all that hardship with her if she had let him. "I'm sorry, Cam."

Camden stood up. "Nothing to be sorry about, is there?"

"For what happened to us over a decade ago."

"That. It's over. Let's move on, right?"

"Right."

"You don't look sure, Iris. That's funny, isn't it? You were so sure last night that it was over between us. I bought it."

Iris didn't know what to say. She had believed—until now—that it had been the right thing for her and Camden to break up.

But today.

Today they had spent hours together searching for news about Bianca in the local community, and being with Camden had brought back a lot of memories of how she had enjoyed being with him.

It seemed to her that eleven years ago, her own inability to handle a life crisis had caused her to push Camden away.

What if God had intended for Camden to help her through that family tragedy?

What if Camden could have been an asset rather than an interference?

She would never know now.

"Iris?" Camden asked gently. "You need to be okay, or else I'll be worried about you the rest of the afternoon and get into a wreck."

"Huh?"

"Got your attention. Listen, sweetheart. I need to get you all back to the house, and then get back to the search," Camden said. "I don't want to be out all night. We have church in the morning, remember?"

"Yes. Early too. Peggy wants to go to Sunday school."

"So do I. Let me summarize for you. What we had eleven years ago was in the past. You said so yourself that it's old history. I won't lie and tell you it didn't hurt me badly when you left me, but what's done is done. Someday, we'll look back and know that we had a good time."

"Yeah, we did have fun. Two immature kids in college, dating—mostly so we could go get ice cream every afternoon in the soda shop."

"That was probably the biggest reason we dated. It was no fun eating desserts alone."

"You don't believe that."

Camden laughed. "But it's over, like you said, and I believe it now. We've both moved on, and we're only communicating right now because of other people—three little adorable kids who are not even ours."

Camden pulled Iris to her feet.

"What are you doing?" Iris asked.

"I'm going to prove to you that there's nothing left between us." Camden cupped both palms on Iris's cheeks and reached for her lips with his. "Watch this. We're going to feel nothing."

At first, Iris was startled. It happened so quickly.

Then she was surprised at herself when her own lips relaxed. Camden deepened the kiss.

Eventually, he lifted his eyes to look at hers. "I guess I was wrong."

Iris's face warmed considerably.

Camden's thumb stroked her chin, her jawline, the base of her ear. He pulled her closer a second time and gently kissed away the rest of her tension. He would have kept at it, but Iris stepped back.

"Maybe that was a mistake," she said.

"Was it?" Camden's voice was barely audible.

"Old history, remember?"

"I believed you when you said that. But it doesn't look like we ever truly left each other."

Somewhere in her heart, Iris knew that he was right.

They hadn't left each other.

After all these years.

CHAPTER FIFTEEN

"What a lovely family," someone declared as she passed by Iris and Camden with three kids in tow going up the ramp to the riverboat where Riverside Chapel held its Sunday services.

Iris was too busy to correct her. Griffin's stroller was heavy, and she had to push it up this unfamiliar ramp. It was her first visit to Camden's church, right in the middle of the most touristy part of Savannah, where everybody was.

Well, truth be told, most of them were tourists and visitors.

She would be surprised if anyone here knew her from high school other than a handful of people—including Ming and his sister Heidi, who was now the pastor's wife. Those two had gone to the University of Georgia, as Iris recalled.

Yes, and if Tamsyn Pendegrast was around, she might remember Iris too, though they had been in different grades at Savannah High.

Someone else going up the ramp pointed to Griffin, making gurgling noises in his stroller. "Oooh, the baby looks like his daddy."

Camden coughed.

Iris chuckled.

"We should get paid for babysitting," Camden whispered to Iris.

"A dollar for every diaper we change?"

"I want a dollar too," Peggy said. She was holding Camden's free hand. His other arm carried Sibley.

"I keep forgetting about little ears," Camden said to Iris.

"My ears are not little." Peggy tugged her earlobes.

Iris didn't say anything. They had reached the large doors leading to the dining hall where the service was to be held. It was crowded today.

Camden introduced Iris to a couple of greeters and ushers, and she promptly forgot their names. Abilene was one of them.

And there was Heidi. Oh boy, she was large with child, as Mom would have said—

Mom.

Iris sucked in her breath, trying to hold it all in.

Heidi hugged Iris as best she could with that belly between them.

"So nice to see you again, Iris. I'm sorry about your sister, but hey, we're all praying fervently for a good outcome."

"Thank you." Iris hadn't seen Heidi in a million years, but her friend had a way of making people at ease. Perfect for the role of a pastor's wife.

"You look amazing, Heidi." And Iris meant it. "You haven't changed a bit, except for being expecting. How far along are you?"

"Seven months."

"Getting there. I'll be praying for you."

"Thank you. Come. I'll take you to the nursery." Heidi led them toward the elevator.

Ten minutes of filling out drop-off forms later, Iris and Camden were back in the dining hall.

It turned out that since Camden had been back in town only recently, they were both sort of new. But Camden had friends from four years ago who still remembered him, whereas Iris's old friends from college and high school had mostly left town.

After saying hi to everyone, they found two seats by a window overlooking the Savannah River.

Iris wondered what everyone did for a living. She hated to ask people such a question, but jobs were in the forefront of her thoughts today. She felt a bit desperate that she needed to find work to replace the job she had lost.

She couldn't live on savings for very long. Besides, she had a car payment and that apartment rent money to think about.

She prayed to God that Bianca would be found soon. At some point, Iris had to go home to Jacksonville and deal with her life there.

Her life?

She had come closer to home when she had moved to Jacksonville six months ago. What did that say about her exactly? That she was closer to closure?

Who knows.

Prior to Jacksonville, San Francisco had been her hiding place for years. She had no family there, and it had been a good retreat from the memories of her family tragedy. For the most part, San Francisco had been where she worked and made a living and didn't talk about family.

For now, taking it one day at a time, Iris knew she couldn't leave her nieces and one cutie-pie nephew until Bianca returned to her family.

How could Bianca disappear like that? Had she been abducted?

Iris wouldn't put it past her sister to be negligent, but she was older now, right? Surely a caring mother would be more responsible than abandoning three children, five and under.

A caring mother?

To be sure, Iris hadn't grown up with a selfless Bianca, but then again, the two sisters had been estranged in their adult lives. Having children could change someone, Iris had heard.

Pastor Flores preached his continuing series on how to be a Daniel in a Darius world. This was sermon number twelve or thirteen, apparently.

Iris thought that she should order the rest of the series—or at least listen to them in the church's online archives—so she could catch up. After all, she expected to be attending church here for a few more weeks.

Lord, please don't let it take too long to find Bianca.

She could be dead and gone.

Next to Iris, Camden sat quietly looking at his Bible and listening to the thirty-something-year-old Pastor Flores. He took no notes.

At the end of the sermon about Daniel in the lion's den—which Iris somehow identified with—Pastor Flores asked everyone to bow their heads to pray with him.

His list of prayer requests included one for Bianca.

"We also pray for Bianca Delaney, missing now

for five days. Lord, I ask that You would protect her, wherever she may be, and bring her home safely to her three children and her sister, Iris. I pray that You would give us wisdom to get the community to help us to find her. Please be with the SCMPD as they're working around the clock to bring her home. In Jesus' Name I pray. Amen."

Iris felt a warm hand on hers.

She didn't have to peek to see whose hand it was. She knew it was Camden's right away.

He gave her fingers a light squeeze as he said a loud "amen" along with the congregation.

And he didn't let her hand go even as they said hello to a few people, until they made their way downstairs to the nursery to pick up the little ones, and then to the children's area to pick up Peggy.

Peggy was wearing a paper hat with crayon drawings and haphazard stickers stuck all over it.

"Auntie Ibis." Peggy tugged at her dress. "I like church."

"Well, that's good, because we'll be back tonight," Iris said, adjusting Sibley, whose sleepy head was resting on Iris's shoulder.

"Yay!" Peggy jumped up and down and lost her hat. She put it back on, and now the scotch tape stuck to her hair. "Oweee..."

Iris couldn't help her with Sibley fast asleep in her arms.

Camden parked the baby buggy. He tried to get that hat off Peggy's hair, but the tape was stuck to more clumps now. He whipped out his Swiss Army knife, found a tiny pair of scissors, and snipped off the bits of golden hair to separate the hat from Peggy's head.

"Never a dull moment." Camden put away his tool, leaned toward Iris, and pecked her on the lips before she could ask why he had brought a knife to church.

"Mr. Cam!" Peggy wagged a finger. Her face was stern. "Not in front of the children!"

CHAPTER SIXTEEN

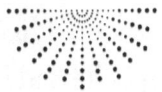

*B*y the time Camden changed Griffin's diaper after lunch, Iris was fast asleep on the old couch in the living room. She looked too peaceful to be disturbed.

Quietly, Camden rocked Griffin until he fell asleep. He placed the baby in his crib in the bedroom, and checked on the other two kids playing quietly on their bedroom floor, surrounded by toys.

They looked like they were about to fall asleep, but Peggy seemed to be trying to stay awake in spite of her frequent yawns.

Camden wasn't sure what he was supposed to do next. He couldn't leave the kids unattended with Iris having gone out like a light as soon as he had driven the troupe home from church.

When the kids had changed out of their Sunday

best, Camden had fed the kids some leftovers that Riverside Chapel church members had provided. He had given Griffin his bottle.

And he had watched Iris sleep.

All right. It's Sunday.

He didn't have to work. He decided he would stay here until Iris woke up. His iPhone charger was in the car, and as long as he had battery, he was good to go. He could be checking his email and doing some research online for hours.

He called Detective Zimmerman and left him a message. He didn't blame the man for not being at work—or at least, not answering his phone—on a Sunday. However, he wanted Zimmerman to know that he was concerned about the missing mother.

In a way, Camden was glad that O'Dell hadn't been assigned to the case. Surely the detective remembered Daljeet and the Oso fiasco from four years ago. Even if O'Dell had forgotten, Camden hadn't. How could he?

The memory made him suddenly nauseous.

He leaned over the kitchen sink, his fists on the counter for support.

He breathed in, felt the bile in his throat, and looked through the cracked and duct-taped window that looked like it had been recently cleaned. It over-looked some sort of fence and the neighbor's house.

There was a window there staring back at him.

He distracted himself by wondering if he should walk over there to ask the neighbors if they had anything else to add to what they had already told the good detective. His extra inquiries wouldn't interfere with the SCMPD investigations. In fact, every bit of extra information helped.

It had been a week since Bianca Delaney had purportedly disappeared. From what Iris had told Zimmerman, Bianca had battled some addictions in the past, but the two sisters had not been close enough for Iris to know if Bianca had had a relapse recently.

Camden ran through a mental list he could do for Iris.

Talk to the neighbors.

Zimmerman had that covered.

Mobilize the community.

Jerome had already started that.

Get the church involved.

He could continue what Pastor Flores had introduced.

Keep in touch with O'Dell—I mean, Zimmerman.

Why did O'Dell's name keep popping up in his head?

Camden was sure that if he ran into O'Dell, he would still blame Camden for letting an international fugitive turn the tables on them and shoot O'Dell's favorite hostage negotiator, Daljeet Gupta, to death.

She had been the best HNT whom Camden had ever known. And he had planned to marry her when that operation was over.

All had gone well, as planned, until nothing did. The fugitive had somehow known they were raiding the safe house in Richmond Hill, outside Savannah.

It had to be an inside job!

Camden punched the Formica countertop with his fists.

Daljeet had paid for the information with her life. Camden's friend, Ming, hadn't fared too much better, having been shot in the gut. Three months of surgeries to repair some internal damages had been followed by more months of rehabilitation.

As for Camden, he had been fired from the bureau.

Thus ended his lifelong dream of being in law enforcement.

Something dripped off Camden's forehead. He didn't realize he was sweating bullets. He closed his eyes so those sweat droplets didn't enter in. Even with his eyes closed, he could see her.

Daljeet on life support.

Daljeet in the morgue.

Daljeet in the ground.

Camden cringed.

"I turned the AC down." Iris's voice was almost a whisper.

Camden swung around. He hid his shaking hands behind him.

"Are you all right?" she asked.

No.

"Want me to get you a glass of cold water?" Iris handed Camden a folded dish towel. When he didn't take it from her, she was about to dab the sweat off his forehead herself.

Camden's hand stopped her hand from reaching him. He took the towel from her. "It's hot in July, isn't it?"

"It's one of the many reasons I left the south and went out west. The humidity just kills."

Kills?

Not a good word for her to say at this time.

Camden's hands shook.

Iris stepped closer.

And closer.

"What are you doing?" Camden's voice was feeble. He didn't want Iris to hear the defeat in his voice, but there was nowhere else he could go. He was backed up against the kitchen sink.

Iris wrapped her arms around his waist and placed her chin on his shoulder. It was a gentle move, and then it was gone. She stepped back.

"That isn't enough," Camden said.

"It's all I have."

"All you want to give?"

"No. There's more I want to give you, but I can't."

"Why not?" Camden wiped his face and neck with the dish towel, then put it down on the counter behind him.

"The timing doesn't feel right."

"We're in this together."

"No, Cam. I'm in this. My sister is missing, not yours. I'm living this. You're not. You can always walk away and return to wherever you came from, and life goes on. I have to deal with the past that keeps coming back to haunt me. Do you know how many times I have relived that—that night...when..."

She fell silent.

"I know, babe." One stride, and his arms were around Iris, holding her tightly. "I know."

The flood of memories returned. The chaos on campus when the news had broken that Mack Delaney had murdered his wife. The weeks of trial and bad publicity that the Delaney family had to endure. The lack of support from their old church for the family covered with the blood of sin.

Where was the forgiveness that Jesus Christ had taught the local church? Camden hadn't been saved then and didn't understand what went on in that church. He never did find out, as the church eventually split and vanished from the Savannah landscape.

What memory is death? Always dark and dreary, it is.

Not only had Iris and Bianca lost their mother, they had also lost their father to the state penitentiary, where he had remained to this day. There was no dialing back that clock.

Death is final. Or is it?

As Camden held Iris in the kitchen, more memories washed over him like a hurricane on Tybee Island, pushing him deeper into the recesses of grief that had pounded him when he had least expected it.

Grief?

Yes, grief.

He had been grieving a bigger loss—more than Daljeet, unfortunately—since that cold, gray day in November, back on the campus of the University of Coastal Georgia on the other side of Savannah, when Iris walked out of his life. He had no idea until the day after their breakup that she had successfully applied for a transfer to another college in San Francisco.

To make it worse, some guy had helped her move across the country. For the life of him, Camden couldn't remember the guy's name. By Christmas that year, Iris was gone.

"You didn't kiss me goodbye," Camden said.

"What?"

"November 1 7, eleven years ago."

"We were young and immature, Cam. If we had married then, we'd be divorced by now."

Camden widened his eyes. "You really think so?"

Iris shrugged. "Neither of us knew what it meant to have a lifelong love."

"And we do now?"

"I don't know. Do we?"

Camden kept her in his arms. No way was he going to let this opportunity pass.

His fingers feathered her cheek. So soft. So Iris.

He lowered his lips—

A shriek startled him.

He and Iris both looked in the same direction.

There was little Peggy, glaring up at them, her clenched fists on her little waist, her chest heaving up and down. "What do you want, Mr. Cam?"

Her eyes were fiery, that little brat.

Camden tried to remain calm. "What do you mean?"

"Fancy asking a five-year-old what she means." Iris chuckled.

Peggy stomped one bare foot, then another. "They all do that to Mommy!"

"Do what, Peggy?" Camden asked as Iris tried to wiggle away from him. He let her go reluctantly.

"Hug her like you did Auntie Ibis."

"Really?" Camden looked at Iris. "And?"

"Sometimes Mommy told them to stop, but they didn't."

Iris wiped the tears from her own eyes. "When they didn't stop hugging your mommy, do you remember what she did?"

"Mommy pointed a squirt gun at them."

"A what?" Camden instinctively reached for the iPhone in his pocket. He had Zimmerman on speed dial, but he had to let Peggy finish talking.

"Don't you know what a squirt gun is?" Peggy tipped her head at him. "Mine is a Super Soaker. Don't you have a squirt gun, Mr. Cam?"

"Of course, I do. Now tell me, Peggy, what color is Mommy's squirt gun?" Camden asked.

"It's black, but when she squirted it, no water came out."

"Does it make a lot of noise?"

"Oh yes, it did." Peggy's eyes were saucer huge. "How did you know, Mr. Cam?"

"I might have heard that sort of squirt gun before. Can you tell me where she was the last time that happened?"

Peggy pointed in the direction of Bianca's bedroom.

Camden stepped around Iris and Peggy as Iris made a beeline for her niece, sweeping her up in her arms and weeping.

Peggy patted her aunt's head. "There, there, Auntie Ibis. It's going to be all right."

The scene was not lost on Camden.

CHAPTER SEVENTEEN

*C*amden opened the door to Bianca's room. The SCMPD had been in here Thursday, but their search had focused on the possible string of men coming through this house.

Camden was not privy to what Zimmerman had found beyond grocery receipts, parking tickets, bank statements, and junk mail. They had photographed or carted off whatever they needed.

What else was there to see here then?

Camden scanned the room. It was painted in dull colors, mostly beige and brown, which seemed unusual to Camden if Bianca was carrying on some sort of illicit business in here. There was a water bed in the middle of it. Up against a wall was an IKEA wardrobe with frosted-glass sliding doors on it.

Camden used his elbow to push it open. Inside were men's and women's clothes.

"What are you looking for?" Iris stood at the bedroom door, Sibley on one hip. Peggy was standing behind her, afraid to enter the room.

"Something I can ask Zimmerman about." Camden walked along the walls of the small room. He pushed back the heavy drapes, too expensive for this room. The afternoon sun seared through the windows and onto the scratched parquet floor.

Iris stepped into the bedroom, Peggy in tow. "Peggy, could you tell Mr. Cam where you saw Mommy point the squirt gun?"

"In the bathroom," Peggy said feebly. "She was coming out of the shower."

Iris blinked.

Camden saw that fleeting pain in her eyes. All else forgotten, he crossed the space between them and squeezed her hand, being careful not to give her another hug. A simple hug had triggered Peggy's memories.

He wondered what else that poor little kid had seen and experienced at such a young, innocent age.

"I wasn't trying to listen." Peggy sounded earnest. "But Giffey was crying, and I came here to get Mommy."

"It's okay, hon," Iris said.

Camden squatted down so that he was eye to eye with Peggy. "Who was here with Mommy?"

"He said he's not giving her any more money." Tears flowed. "That's why if you buy one of Pink's kittens for one million dollars, Mr. Cam, Mommy wouldn't need to ask him for money."

If Camden remembered correctly, the asking price was five million dollars, not one, but he wasn't about to start an argument.

"Do you remember the man's name, Peggy?" he asked instead, even as he dialed Zimmerman's number.

Peggy shrugged.

Camden wasn't sure whether he should push harder, but it looked like Peggy was about to shut out the world and return to her kiddie wonderland.

His eyes met Iris's.

"Peggy?" Iris asked.

"Don't know!" Peggy ran out of the room.

Iris, still carrying Sibley, followed her, and Camden followed Iris.

They found Peggy climbing into her bed in the pink-and-yellow bedroom she shared with Sibley. She held her yellow smiley purse as she pulled the covers up over her neck. Part of the purse rested on the pillow next to her.

"I'm taking a nap now. Wake me up when it's

time to go back to church, Auntie Ibis," Peggy said, drifting off. "I like church..."

~

"*Y*ou cleaned the house from top to bottom, except this bedroom?" Detective Zimmerman said as he stood in Bianca's room.

He was surrounded by crime scene investigators. They were not collecting fingerprints as they had done that on Thursday.

Earlier, Camden had told Iris that they were going to upturn the house, looking for gunshot residues and other telltale signs of foul play.

This time, because of the new evidences in Bianca's photographs, they would also look for blood stains, body fluids, and some other things that Camden had mentioned that Iris had promptly forgotten.

Still, Iris appreciated how Camden had tried to prepare her for things.

Thoughtful, as always.

"I wasn't sure how Bianca wanted her room cleaned, so I left it the way it was." She stepped out of the way as more investigators poured into the hallway.

"Let's talk out there." Zimmerman led the way.

For someone who had to come out here to Tybee Island on his Sunday off, he seemed pretty nonchalant about it. "It's a bit of luck, isn't it?"

Iris walked beside the detective. "No, sir. I don't think it's luck. I think it's the providence of God to preserve the evidence for you to collect."

Zimmerman's jaw dropped. "You seriously believe that, Miss Delaney?"

"Life and death are pretty serious issues. Without God, I don't know how we would make it."

"Speaking for yourself."

"Right. Speaking for my family. I suppose you do know our history."

Iris followed Zimmerman out of the house to the front entrance, where Camden and the kids were waiting for her.

It was quite a sight for her to see Camden leaning against the siding of the house, holding Griffin in his arms and feeding him a bottle of formula.

He looked like a dad.

"...tragic. I'm sorry." Zimmerman had more to say, it seemed.

"Sorry about what?" Iris asked.

"Your family. You were saying—"

Camden cut him off. "I suppose we all have to clear out of here."

"Right. We'll be done in a few hours, if not less."

Zimmerman nodded. "I see your nieces are ready to go."

There beside Camden, Peggy and Sibley waited, holding hands. Sibley was sucking her thumb, as per usual.

Peggy held her yellow purse with smiley stickers on it. She was still in the same cotton dress she had worn to church this morning that Mrs. Untermeyer had picked out from her basement and had given to Iris on Saturday night when they picked up the kids from her house. It had been her daughter Amy's church clothes when she was about Peggy's age, but the classic style didn't show any age. Besides, it was machine washable. Score!

Iris nearly smiled if not for the irony of it. Two pretty daughters, waiting to be driven back to evening church—was it still Sunday?—and their mother couldn't be here to see it.

"Let's go to evening church, girls." Iris dug into her purse. "You still have the key to this house, Detective?"

Zimmerman nodded. "Until the case is solved."

"Please lock up, yes?"

"Yes, ma'am."

"Thank you." Iris stepped toward the baby carrier on the floor. She popped open the five-point harness for Camden to put Griffin in. She watched him burp the baby over his broad shoulder before buckling him in.

She was about to ask Camden not to forget the diaper bag, when she saw that he had it over his shoulder.

"I'm impressed, Cam," she said.

"About what?"

"You fed the baby, burped him, carried him, and didn't forget the diaper bag."

"I had young nephews and nieces once, remember?"

Yes, Iris remembered that Camden's older brother, Bryce, had a passel of new kids back when Iris and Camden were still in college. "I don't recall them letting you babysit."

"I never did. Bryce's oldest girl from his first marriage babysat her younger siblings a lot."

Iris looked alarmed.

"I just watched what they all did." Camden snapped the baby carrier into its base at the backseat of Iris's car.

"No kidding. You're a natural then."

"A natural what?"

"A natural...uh...dad."

Camden closed the back passenger door and stood awfully close to Iris. "You're a pretty natural mom yourself, sweetheart."

CHAPTER EIGHTEEN

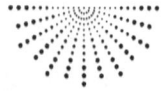

*S*izzling didn't even begin to describe the Monday afternoon furnace that was Bianca's backyard on Tybee Island. The chain-link fence surrounding the small yard seemed to divide the weedy patch of property from the tree-lined neighbors' houses on both sides of the property, as if this slither of space had been a builder's afterthought.

No trees. No shade.

Camden felt his body cook in his own sweat in the midnineties temperature.

Nonetheless, he was happy mowing the lawn to save Iris from having to do it herself.

Yep, for Iris.

Camden made up his mind that this time he would do things differently. When he had been twenty-three years old, letting Iris go meant he could date other people. He hadn't been serious then, even though he had known that Iris was the only girl he had ever loved.

Fast-forward eleven years—almost twelve now—things had changed.

Today, he was surer of himself, what he wanted in life, where he was going.

It helped tremendously that he had the way, the truth, and the life in Jesus Christ.

Does Iris get that? I'm a different man now.

The high decibels of the lawnmower motor was all he could hear in the great southern outdoors as Camden pushed across the lawn. He had borrowed the lawnmower from Mrs. Untermeyer because Bianca didn't have one.

Seriously, Iris. I've changed!

The small yard only half-covered with grass made light work for Camden. He finished mowing the lawn and rolled the lawnmower back to his pickup truck. He tried to handle the lawnmower carefully. Mrs. Untermeyer loved this thing.

Borrowed things.

Borrowed time.

Camden had been praying about taking that job Bryce had offered him at the gun shop and shooting range. It paid well and provided stability for him if he decided to raise a family.

Working as a PI had its perks and perils. For one thing, life was never dull. Tonight he had to go undercover with one of Helen Hu's associates. Ming still received a lot of work from Helen Hu, and this one, if played right, would lead them to Frankfurt.

Yes, Germany.

No, I don't want to go.

All Camden wanted to do was to stay with Iris.

Wherever she went, he would go.

He had mentioned that shooting range job to Ming. Ming didn't have an opinion about it, except that Camden should pray about the ramifications of doing two full-time jobs.

But first, he had to at least finish one project at Savannah River Investigations, and that didn't include searching for Iris's sister.

After Camden hoisted the lawnmower onto the flatbed of the truck, he tied it down with a bungee cord and closed the tailgate. He retrieved his duffel bag from the front seat of the truck and went inside the house after taking off his grass-covered shoes and socks outside the front door.

Iris was in the kitchen, washing out Griffin's baby bottle.

"The bathroom is at the end of the hallway." Iris dried her hands on a dish towel.

"Are you saying I stink?" Camden joked as he

opened the refrigerator to get something cold to drink. Nothing there.

When he turned around, Iris was standing in front of him with a cold glass of water, hand extended.

"Thank you."

"Did you bring a change of clothes?" Iris wiped down the kitchen table.

"Yes, you told me to."

"Nice of you to listen."

"I should've listened to you a long time ago, Iris." Camden refilled his glass with water from the tap. "Remember when we were dating in college? You told me many times about how Jesus was going to change my life, and I didn't listen."

"Well, my family turned out to be hypocrites."

"Not your fault." Camden's eyes met hers. "But you planted the seed, Iris. I got saved."

"God worked it out, didn't He? I'm glad. You do have a nice church. Good people. Good preacher."

"Yep. Hard to find a good church nowadays." Camden finished drinking his water, and put the glass down on the countertop.

"Don't slip on the rubber duckies in the bathtub," Iris said. "There should be some clean towels in the cabinet underneath the sink."

"Thanks, but I brought my own towel." Camden made his way down the hallway.

After the master bedroom, he passed by a smaller room that looked like a storage closet. The door was open. Inside, up against the windowless wall, was a cot with a pillow and a ruffled blanket on it. At the foot of the cot was a carry-on on the floor, its lid leaning against the wall. Clothes were sticking out of it, a couple of women's blouses and a pair of shorts.

"The bathroom is this way, Mr. Cam," a tiny voice said.

Camden looked at the pint-sized usher pointing away from what seemed to be where Iris had been sleeping. "Thank you."

"Mr. Cam?"

"Yes, Miss Peggy?"

"Do you like Auntie Ibis?"

"Very much."

"I don't know if she likes you."

Camden didn't want to read too much into it. "What do you mean?"

"Every time we say a blessing before we eat, she always prays for you, but she cries as she prays."

Camden's heart fell. "She does?"

"That's what I just said. Pay attention, Mr. Cam. Don't they teach you that in school?"

"It's been a while since I was in school."

Peggy shook her head. "Maybe you should go back."

"To school?"

"Yes."

Camden had no words.

"I'm going to school, you know," Peggy volunteered.

"You are?" *This is interesting.* "This fall?"

Peggy shrugged. "Mommy said I have to wear a...you nee...you need something..."

"Uniform?" Camden asked.

"Yes, yes!"

"Is this kindergarten or first grade?"

"Kiddie garden!" Peggy jumped up and down. "I'm going to play in the garden all day. It will be fun!"

"Do you know what color your uniform will be?"

"Pretty colors!" And Peggy skipped off to her la-la land, leaving Camden standing there in the hallway.

So. Which schools in town required kinder-garteners to wear uniforms?

And how could Bianca, on welfare, afford it?

CHAPTER NINETEEN

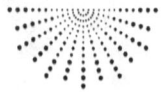

*F*eeling safe when Camden La Salle was around wasn't something Iris had expected, after all these years. Even though he was still in the shower, the fact that he was in this very house with them put Iris at ease.

She wasn't sure why.

She had dumped him unceremoniously so long ago.

In her own defense, she had been young. Nineteen and not ready for a long-term commitment. She felt bad that she had used her family tragedy as an excuse to leave Camden.

She was now back to square one. Her ground zero.

Would she run away again?

She heard a little wail. Griffin. She left the

kitchen and went to get the baby. People said that a baby ruled the family's daily schedule, but she hadn't understood that until now.

She picked up Griffin, sweaty in his onesie. The fan was on, but he was still hot. Was he sick?

Iris touched Griffin's forehead. Not too warm. She looked around for a thermometer but could not find any.

She checked Griffin's diaper. It wasn't too wet, but she decided to change it anyway.

Iris was picking up a diaper from one of the shelves under the changing table, when Camden walked in.

His hair was damp. A neatly folded bath towel was on top of the zipped-up duffel bag, its handles wrapping around the towel to keep it from falling off.

Camden approached her. He smelled like Dial soap.

"You'll never guess what Peggy said to me." His voice was low.

Iris raised an eyebrow.

"She's going to kindergarten where they wear uniform."

Iris froze in the middle of swapping out Griffin's diapers. "On welfare?"

"That's what I want to know. I'll keep you posted."

"Sounds like something you might want to talk to Zimmerman about."

"Will do that too. But sometimes, you know, people would rather talk to a civilian."

"You'll still have to tell them you're a PI."

"I'll say I'm a friend of the family."

"Are you?" Iris teared up. She tried to focus on Griffin, get him into a clean diaper.

"I want to be more than a friend of the family, but we'll have to get through this crisis first."

Iris nodded.

"After this, maybe we could..."

Iris didn't know—didn't want to know—what Camden was getting at.

Camden cleared his throat. "Maybe we could catch up. Have a cup of coffee?"

"Coffee."

"Yes. Maybe here or in Jacksonville, if you decide to go home."

"Home."

"Is that a statement or a question?"

"I don't know where we go from here, Cam."

"But the other day—Saturday—something happened, didn't it?" Camden's voice seemed too earnest to Iris.

"A memory, Cam. It was only a memory." *There we go. Push him away.*

"Was it?"

Iris picked up Griffin. She wasn't sure what she wanted. On the one hand, she wanted to be with Camden. On the other hand, she was too overwhelmed by the current situation to think straight.

"I—uh, I need more faith, Cam."

"We all do." Camden followed her out of the baby's room.

"Let's talk another time, Cam. You need to go to work."

Camden's shoulders dropped. "All right. I'm going to be up all night, and I won't be any good tomorrow. But Jerome promised me he'll call you if they have new information."

"And I'll let you know if anyone else contacts me on social media."

"Yeah. Just text me." Camden sighed. "I have a bad feeling about you and the kids staying here."

"You said that multiple times, but Detective Zimmerman says they're following leads out there. Out there, Cam. This house doesn't seem to be a target. Or else, he would have told us to move, or sent Garcia or someone to keep an eye on us."

"Maybe Bianca has taken her pursuers away from her kids."

Iris wiped her forehead with the back of her hand. "I don't know, Cam. At this point, I can believe anything. For all we know, Bianca could walk in any minute now."

"We're still praying—and everyone at church is praying—that she will come home safely."

Iris tried to remain positive. "Maybe she just needs space."

"Well, she'll have space in eighteen years when Griffin goes to college." Camden headed for the door. He stopped. Walked back to Iris.

He looked like he was about to say something, but wordlessly, and with a smooth slide of his free hand, he pulled Iris and the baby toward himself.

Camden's face was warm on Iris's cheek. She closed her eyes and tasted the lip balm on his lips. She didn't want to pull away, and she didn't know why.

When Camden released her lips, he smiled. "Still there."

Iris didn't reply.

"We do have something going on." Camden touched her elbow. "Don't worry. I'm not going to kiss and run."

You mean, like I did? Iris gulped.

"I loved you then, Iris. I love you now, and I will love you always."

Iris's lips quivered. She pursed them so Camden couldn't see.

"Speaking of running...uh-oh. Famous last words." Camden laughed, and Griffin cooed. "I do have to run...but to work! I'll call you later, okay?"

He ruffled gurgling Griffin's mop of curly hair and rushed out the front door without another word.

Iris heard the pickup truck come to life. She locked the door and peeked out the window until she couldn't see the truck down the road or hear it anymore.

She was about to turn away, when the reflection of a man's face appeared in the window.

Iris screamed.

CHAPTER TWENTY

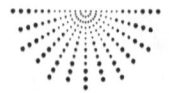

"Gimme my s-son!" His voice slurred. He could barely keep his feet on the ground as he staggered back and forth, one hand with dirty fingernails waving a gun at Iris.

His eyes and his pasty face were the first things Iris had seen reflected off the window. So distracted had she been with Camden driving off that she hadn't realized another adult was in the house with her.

The girls!

She glanced beyond the man, in the direction of the hallway. She held her breath when she saw Peggy peeking out of her bedroom door—

"I'm talking to you!" He spat out chewing tobacco at her.

It smelled like more than that, but Iris had

nothing to compare it with, though it faintly smelled almost like the house the first time she had arrived that Wednesday night.

Lord Jesus, help me!

The living room felt warm. Iris clutched Griffin tightly against her chest, as if letting him go would be to send the baby to his death.

The man came toward her again. He tried to reach for Griffin with a hand that shook so badly that Iris could hardly count the scars and bruises up and down that arm.

"I said, gimme my son!"

Iris didn't move. "Griffin is a good boy."

"T-takes after his m-mother."

"I changed his diaper," Iris said as calmly as she could.

"G-good."

"He had a nap," Iris added. "He hasn't eaten though. May I feed him?"

"How long is it going to t-take?" He was positively shivering now.

Meanwhile, Iris was sweating buckets. She breathed in deeply, slowly, all the while praying for God to send angels to protect her and the three children.

"Not long. Just have to mix the formula. Have a seat. What's your name, sir?"

Her iPhone was in the pocket of her shorts, but

she could not reach it. Somehow she had to be able to get to it, dial 911, call for help, and protect the children in the process.

"Not saying..." He swayed.

Iris could see that his pupils were dilated. He needed a fix.

Could that explain why he had asked for Griffin?

But why this baby? Unless...

Of course.

Sell the baby. Make some money. Buy some drugs.

"Please sit down. I'll feed your son, and then we can go." Iris knew then and there that God had given her the strength to speak.

More than that, God had arrested her fear.

What time I am afraid, I will trust in thee.

Camden's recitation of Psalm 56:3 wrapped around her like a Kevlar jacket and pushed her to a new resolve.

She had to keep the kids safe from this druggie.

Or die trying.

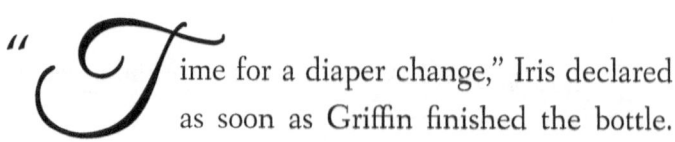

"**T**ime for a diaper change," Iris declared as soon as Griffin finished the bottle.

She had put the formula in the biggest baby bottle Bianca had for Griffin, hoping that it would buy time.

The baby had cooperated, downing at least two-thirds of the bottle.

Across the armchair, Griffin's armed dad was jittery and twitchy.

Iris prayed continuously that God would hold back his trigger finger because he was waving the weapon too carelessly about. The moment he put that down, Iris was going to retaliate.

However, she had no firearm to take him out—

Whoa.

She hadn't spoken like that since college.

She blinked. No time to dig up old wounds now. That had been a long-lost career dream of hers, buried in the pit of despair along with the other deaths—of family, of futures, of faith...

Faith?

No, she had backslidden in her fervor for God, but she had not entirely lost her faith in God.

Besides, as Pastor Flores had preached on Sunday at Riverside Chapel, God had a hold on Daniel in the lion's den. God had not let him go. Daniel was safe in His everlasting arms.

Just as I have safety in Christ.

"May I change your son's diaper?" Iris asked

because it seemed that Griffin's dad had not heard her the first time.

He flicked his gun at her. "Let's g-go."

Iris wasn't surprised that he knew where the baby's room was. He had clearly been in this house before. She wondered if this was the same man that Bianca had pointed her "squirt gun" at.

Camden had said the SCMPD was still working on ballistic reports. They had found no spent casings in the house. Iris didn't know how Camden came about that piece of information since Detective Zimmerman had been tightlipped about everything.

Still, here was a gunman. Exhibit A.

Iris took her time to reach the baby's room, the gun to her back.

Lord Jesus, please take care of these babies, no matter what happens to me.

"Hurry up!" Griffin's dad pushed the barrel end of his weapon into her spine.

Iris wondered how she was going to call 911 on her iPhone. Siri was loud. Whoever answered the phone at the other end would speak audibly. Whatever vocal sounds there were, Griffin's dad would hear them all.

Then she remembered the app she had installed a year ago. Did it still work? A couple of single friends at work had told her about this app where a person in distress could call 911 one way. The app would transmit the location and record the scenario live without giving away the location of—

Ping!

"What's that?" Griffin's dad snapped.

Ping!

Iris knew she had to make up a story. "The baby timer. No worries."

"A baby timer?"

"Yes, it tells me it's diaper time and feeding time and sleeping time and—"

"Shut up and just change the baby."

Iris grabbed a flannel baby blanket and a couple of diapers and tossed them at the end of the changing table. Then she placed Griffin gently on the covered foam pad, leaning over him to smile and coo at him.

"Hurry!"

"Shhhh... Don't make him cry," Iris scolded.

Griffin's dad—Iris wondered if he was truly the baby's dad—looked startled that he had just been reprimanded.

"You want him quiet, right?" Iris asked.

He nodded his head. He leaned against the doorframe.

The split second his eyes fluttered, Iris slid her iPhone from her pocket to the changing table under the pile of flannel blanket and diapers, pushing the emergency app button at the bottom of the screen.

The gunman's eyes opened. He pointed the gun at her. "Change him, and let's go."

"Please don't point your gun at my baby," Iris said loudly.

"Not your baby!"

"My sister's son...and yours." Iris took her time. "Where are we going?"

"Shut up, you b—"

"Auntie Ibis?" a small voice called out to Iris.

Iris's heart leapt into her throat. She was still wiping down Griffin, but her head turned.

Peggy stood at the door to the nursery, her yellow smiley purse over an arm. She glanced at Iris and then at the gunman. "Mr. Simon, where's Mommy?"

"I don't know!"

Ah, his name is Simon.

Iris hoped that the dispatcher had heard every word.

"If you want money, I can give you some," Iris offered. "Just tell me where Bianca is."

"Haven't s-seen her." His face hardened. "I'm better than him."

"Him? Who?" Iris spoke calmly.

"Her new boyfriend, that's who. But she's coming back to me. I guarantee—"

"Mommy's coming back?" Peggy inched forward.

Simon kicked her. Peggy jumped back. Held on to the door.

"Peggy!" Iris worked the Velcro as fast as she could, snapped the onesie back on Griffin, and held him up. "Please don't hurt her. Her mom would be worried sick."

"She's already sick. Leyshon's giving her... See if I care!" Simon laughed. "Serves her right!"

What did he mean—

Who is Leyshon?

Simon pointed his weapon in Iris's face. "Be done. Let's go!"

Iris braved herself. "Where are we going, may I ask?"

"No, you may not!"

"I need to know how many diapers to bring, how much formula to pack. If it's a long trip..."

"Sh-short trip. They have formula."

They? They who?

The unthinkable popped into Iris's mind, a confirmation of an earlier suspicion.

And she knew that she could not possibly let Simon take Griffin—or any of the other kids—at all.

If she could get him distracted...

"Hurry!" Simon now directed his weapon back at Iris.

Iris felt no fear.

Whenever I'm afraid, I will trust in You, Lord...

She walked slowly out of the nursery. Her free hand reached for Peggy's.

She wondered where Sibley was. The playroom —bedroom—door was closed.

She wouldn't put it past Peggy to ask Sibley to stay inside the playroom, where it was safe.

Safe? How safe was a hollow wooden door against bullets?

Peggy tugged at Iris's arm, and Iris felt a strap touch her wrist. She dared not glance down, but she felt smooth plastic in her palm, and sticky paper in her fingers.

It seemed to her that Peggy had given her that yellow smiley purse.

What—

The purse was heavy.

Too heavy.

A thought drew across Iris's mind, and she tried to remain calm.

"Do you want me to put Griffin in his car seat?" she asked Simon.

He nodded.

Simon says yes.

"Then please point the gun in another direction."

Simon laughed. He yanked Peggy's hair, and

now his gun was on Peggy's head. "Put the baby in. Now!"

The car seat was by the front door, next to a couple of pairs of sandals and flip-flops.

Iris prayed again that her iPhone app had called the police and that she wouldn't get the kids hurt with what she was about to do.

Would it be too much to ask God for a loaded weapon?

And help me remember how to use it.

"Uncle Joe?"

Everyone turned toward the voice. Sibley was standing in the hallway, stroking a kitten in her arms.

This was no time for Iris to ask why Sibley called the gunman *Uncle Joe* and Peggy called him *Mr. Simon.*

"Hey, Sibley." Simon pushed Peggy away.

"Did you bring the mammon buns?" Sibley let the kitten down. It disappeared into the kitchen.

"Sorry, Sibley. I forgot," Simon said. "Next time?"

Red alert! We have a deranged gunman with manners!

While Simon was still talking to Sibley about cinnamon buns, Iris faced them, her left hand reaching behind the car seat where she had placed Peggy's yellow smiley purse. Quickly and quietly, she unzipped the purse and saw a clear plastic bag.

The slide on the handgun faced up, but she didn't have to read the golden inscription.

She recognized the Glock 26 right away.

It was hers.

CHAPTER TWENTY-ONE

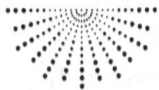

Once upon a time, Dad had told Iris that using a firearm was like riding a bike or swimming laps. One never forgot what to do. Her shooting instructor through high school and that grievous first year in college, Dad had been the marksman to listen to.

But not to follow.

His fiery temper had been his downfall, a frequent nightmare to his wife and two daughters.

Eventually, the SCMPD had known the family by name, and Dad had lost his license to carry.

That hadn't stopped Dad from pointing a rifle in Mom's face that summer night when school was out, and Mom had the worst migraine in her life.

It had also been her last night on earth.

Iris's eye stung now as she saw Dad lift that rifle

he had taught her to use since she had been twelve or thirteen.

The rest was a loud blur.

Later, her counselors would explain to her that she had not been expected to choose between her parents, that even though she could have shot her dad to save her mom, the fact that she hadn't meant there had been no blood on her hands.

She hadn't killed anyone.

Yes, I did.

I froze. Mom died.

Could Iris have stopped the murder?

Well, her first-place finish at the intervarsity marksmanship competition—way back when—said she could. She had only been seventeen, the youngest sharpshooter in the history of the contest.

In college, she had won several more championships, earning this golden Glock she now held in her hands.

As if on cue, Griffin wailed.

"Make him stop!" Simon yelled at Iris.

"Okay, okay!" Iris glanced at him as he returned to speaking with Sibley about cinnamon buns.

Still squatting down and facing Simon and the girls, Iris made a big deal of adjusting a baby blanket over Griffin, even though it was hot summertime, while her other hand slid the Glock out of the ziplock bag.

Pointless if it has no bite.

She checked the magazine.

Loaded.

She turned toward the gunman, while tucking the Glock into her back waistband.

Ready.

The last time she had loaded this Glock was...

That night.

If she had been more decisive...

It didn't have to be this Glock, really. She could have taken Dad out with any firearm she could grab in Dad's gun safe that night while waiting for the police to arrive.

But she hadn't been decisive enough.

One second too late, and Mom was gone.

Now I have to decide again.

One thing bothered her. How did Bianca get ahold of the Glock? It had been stolen from her glove compartment so many years ago. Iris had reported it...

Somehow Bianca had kept it all these years.

How could it be?

Twelve to thirteen feet away from Iris and Griffin in his car seat, a distracted Simon was saying more things to Sibley.

It was then that Iris saw how muddy Simon's sports shoes were. The laces were practically black, but there was brown and red mud all over his shoes, disappearing into his dirty jeans, ripped in a few places.

Peggy walked toward Simon, startling him. He pointed his gun at the girl, but his legs went another way. He tried to straighten himself—

"Peggy, duck!" Iris screamed.

"Where?" Peggy screamed back.

Sigh!

"Drop and roll, girls!"

From the corner of Iris's eye, she saw Peggy yank Sibley hard as they both went down on the carpet.

Above them, the confused, drug-addled Simon roared, his shaking hands twisting his gun this way and that. He aimed it at Iris.

It was all it took for her to react.

CHAPTER TWENTY-TWO

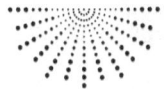

*T*hree shots.

And Iris had missed two out of those three. Missed the vital organs she should have aimed at—brain and heart. She hadn't because she wanted Simon alive.

Bianca had been missing for at least seven days. Detective Zimmerman hadn't shared any information with her or Camden—or Ming and his PI firm, for that matter—for legal reasons.

The community search had begun on Friday but had yielded nothing to add to the SCMPD investigations.

Then Simon showed up at Bianca's house. That had been unexpected.

Once again, Camden's instinct had been right. By the grace of God, Iris and the children were safe.

If the children had not been in danger, Iris would have tried to get Simon to talk more.

But now he was dead.

The curb beneath her was still warm into the evening, and probably filthy and covered with germs, but she was too exhausted to care. She crossed her long legs and shifted Griffin to her left arm.

Griffin cooing in her arms told her that perhaps she had been wrong about missing her shots and her dangerous attempt to engage a drug addict brandishing a weapon at three little kids.

If the SCMPD and Special Weapons and Tactics team hadn't arrived when they had, there was no telling what kind of slaughter there might have been.

Thank You, Lord.

The three kids were safe. The paramedics had checked them out. Not a scratch.

She stretched her right arm all the way across Sibley's shoulders to her right, patting Peggy's head.

"Auntie Ibis?" Peggy asked.

"Yes?"

"Will they give me back my smiley purse?"

"If they don't, we'll get you a new one."

"With stickers?"

Iris nodded. "We'll get you some new ones, and you can stick them on the purse yourself."

"What about Blue and Pink?" Peggy was crying now.

"The nice officers said they would round them up for us."

"Nice? Are you sure they are nice? They weren't nice when they made a lot of noise and scared Mr. Simon."

Iris felt sorry for poor little Peggy, getting the event all turned upside down. Someday, she might explain to her niece who the bad guys were. For now, Iris let it go.

"Good news. We rounded up your cats." Officer Garcia came over to give them some bottled water.

"Yippee!" Peggy jumped up.

Next to her, Sibley tried to mimic her older sister but fell back onto the grass. Peggy rolled next to her, and they laughed.

Officer Garcia sat down on the curb next to Iris. "That shot was gold. You plucked that piece right off him."

"You saw it?"

"I saw the whole thing, ma'am. We had binocs."

"I'm glad you all arrived in time." Iris tried to keep her voice even, but she was slowly losing it.

Yep. Thank God for the SCMPD.

"Why did Detective Zimmerman tell us it was okay for us to stay in the house?" Iris asked.

"Because all leads were taking us away from

Tybee," Garcia said without hesitating. "It's part of a larger scale investigation. That's all I can tell you."

That was plenty.

"If we had any reason to believe that you and the kids should have been taken to a safe place, we would have," Garcia continued. "But there were no threats against you or the kids."

"And the fingerprints?"

"Today is Monday, right. We got the prints just Thursday, and got the DNA evidence on Sunday—oh, that was yesterday. Everything takes time and money."

"Ah, the PD has higher priorities."

"Not necessarily, Miss Delaney. I'm just saying that we did not believe you or the kids were in any danger."

"Simon said we were."

"The ironies of life." Garcia stood up. "I can tell you that after you speak with Detective Zimmerman, you need to clear out of here, because a man was shot and killed in there, and we'll be all over the place all night."

Simon—also known as Uncle Joe or Griffin's dad—hadn't gone down when Iris hit his arm. His handgun had flown right off, and his hand had bled badly, but he had screamed and struggled to get the gun from the floor with his other hand.

Yeah, Iris hadn't wanted him dead. She wanted him to tell the SCMPD where Bianca was.

But she had angered the drug addict even more by missing. So Iris shot him again, but by then she was shaking so badly she couldn't see what she was aiming at except center mass.

Simon hadn't gone down until the SWAT took him out.

If Dad were there, he would have aimed for the head. Dad had been trained for it. Iris had never been in the service to know and make such decisions.

Decisions.

The very thing that Camden had prayed for her.

Nonetheless, the decisions had been made for her by the SCMPD SWAT team.

Iris closed her eyes. She could see it. Hear it. Smell it.

The windows behind Iris had shattered as Simon instantly collapsed onto the grimy carpet. Iris began crawling toward Peggy and Sibley, huddling and sobbing on the carpet between the living room couch and the kitchen.

Just then, the front door splintered and fell in as heavy boots swarmed into the little living room that had seen so much in its existence.

Iris had squinted at the bright lights that came in from the outside through the shattered door.

Doesn't Detective Zimmerman have a spare key to the house?

CHAPTER TWENTY-THREE

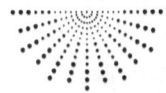

*C*amden jumped out of his pickup truck and zigzagged among patrol vehicles, and SWAT and paramedic trucks, looking for Iris.

Only Iris.

But it was nighttime and the street lights were no good this side of Tybee Island. All around him red and blue flashing lights highlighted bits and pieces of trees and adjacent buildings. It was cloudy tonight, and humid.

Panic gripped Camden when he couldn't see Iris anywhere, until he saw Officer Garcia standing up. It was she who had left a voicemail for him, saying that she was outside Bianca's house waiting for the SWAT team to sweep the house. Detective Zimmerman was on his way there to take a statement from Iris, and if Camden had any more questions, he could ask the man.

As it happened, Camden wouldn't have checked his voicemail if Ming Wei and the undercover team hadn't taken a break. That job at an airport hangar had Camden playing the role of a buyer for a private art collector.

They had aborted tonight's operation because the art thieves had somehow found out that the gallery owner had hired private investigators to track down a Winslow Homer 1892 watercolor painting the thieves had stolen.

At the FBI field office in downtown Savannah, the trio—Ming, Helen, and Camden—and their FBI and SCMPD counterparts had been debriefing their failed operation when Camden checked his email.

And here I am.

Camden's eyes zoomed in to where Officer Garcia was standing. He couldn't see who was behind the patrol vehicle, but in any case, Garcia would know where Iris was.

He didn't have to ask.

Iris was sitting on the curb, looking worn out, cuddling Griffin with one arm. Peggy and Sibley were rolling on the grass behind Iris.

A great relief washed over Camden, in spite of

the feeling that all his energy had drained out of him since the message had come.

"Cam!" Iris burst into tears.

Oh boy. It's going to be tough if she gets this emotional on our wedding day—

Camden startled himself with his own thoughts. He sat down next to Iris and tried to keep himself together before he gave Iris a light squeeze.

Officer Garcia picked up Griffin from Iris and motioned for the two girls to go with her off to another part of the road so that Iris and Camden could have some privacy.

"All is well," Camden said. "Don't worry."

For some reason, Iris started telling him what happened. Camden wasn't sure if she should relive it this soon, but if this was her coping mechanism, then okay. He sat there quietly and listened as attentively as he could, trying not to keep thinking about how beautiful Iris was.

How beautiful she had always been.

And how beautiful she would always be to him.

~

"Looks like it came back to you when you needed it most," Camden said.

"What did?" Iris searched his eyes

in the thick of night, buzzing insects all around them.

Suddenly antsy that she should get the kids and take them someplace safe—away from mosquitoes!—she wanted to get up.

"Skills from your competitive shooting days." Camden pulled her to her feet.

"Past history."

"It's not history if that's our background." Camden didn't let go of her hands. "That's how we met, remember?"

Iris had been a freshman at the University of Coastal Georgia, back when it used to be called Coastal Atlantic College of Georgia.

"I took two years off after high school before I went to college, or else we wouldn't have met," Camden reminded her.

"Well, you also got held back a year after that, though if I remember correctly, you made up for it by taking summer classes."

"You remember more that I'd expected." Camden grinned. "Looking back, I have no idea how I flunked the entire semester."

"I think your brother worked you too hard at the gun range. You had to earn enough money to pay for college, and ironically, you didn't get enough sleep to stay awake through your morning classes."

"Well, the lesson there is not to take any class before noon." Camden laughed.

"Then we would never have met. I only took morning classes."

"We would've still met, really, since we both did competitive shooting, though a lot of good that did— you beat me at regional inter-varsity, and I lost my scholarship."

"Sore loser." Iris had been a competitive shooter since her teenage years, when Dad had entered her into competitions for high schoolers. She had gotten very good at it.

Useless skill...except tonight.

"Do you remember those walks we took on the riverfront?" Camden asked.

"You're still reliving the past?"

"You said that after college you might go into law enforcement."

"Pipe dream."

"You were pretty serious then."

"Things changed, Cam." Iris didn't want to get into that part of her life, a sealed box of bad memories.

"Sins of the fathers are not the sins of the children."

Iris shrugged. "It just didn't work out."

"So you stopped shooting. And you worked secretarial for years."

Iris spotted Detective Zimmerman heading toward them. She began walking.

"We'll talk another time," Camden said.

Iris barely nodded.

To her surprise, Camden didn't leave her side the entire night. He called Mrs. Untermeyer to take in the Delaneys—again. He babysat the kids while Iris answered Zimmerman's questions. He kept the kids occupied and put them into Iris's car so they could sleep if they wanted to.

All the time, his eyes were on her.

She wasn't sure she liked that sort of protectiveness.

But Cam is Cam.

"You haven't been here a week, and all these happened." Zimmerman pocketed his smartphone. "Have you considered maybe applying for a job at SCMPD? Trainees with bachelor's degrees are paid fairly well, especially those with firearms background."

"I'm thinking of doing some work for Mrs. Untermeyer," Iris said.

"Holiday decorating?" Zimmerman smiled. "The SCMPD pays more. Way more."

"But working at Christmastown is low stress."

"Yeah? You should see all the high-stress calls we get during the holidays." Zimmerman chortled.

"How long is the SCMPD training?" Iris didn't know why she asked.

"About six months or so. Not too bad, right?"

"I'll still need a job during that time."

"Well, there's Christmastown to hold you over." Zimmerman sounded serious. "Think about it?"

"Sure."

"All right. If I have more questions, I'll call you."

He started to walk away, when Iris stopped him.

"He's dead. How are you going to find my sister now?" Iris wondered what could have been had they not killed the gunman with the many names.

Then again, if the SWAT sniper hadn't killed him, what could the gunman have done to the little children?

"He's not the only lead. We're still processing the fingerprints from the house."

"How long is that going to take?" Iris asked.

"A few more weeks. If we can't get them in a couple of months, we'll send them to another regional lab in metro Atlanta."

"Months? My sister..."

"You can be sure we're working our hardest, Miss Delaney. We have the 'squirt gun,' as Peggy calls it. We have Mr. Simon—Uncle Joe or whoever —who will provide us with plenty of information."

"He's dead." *Didn't I say that?*

"The dead can speak."

"How long will it take?"

"They have sent the body to the coroner."

"How long?"

"Days, at most a few weeks."

"My sister could be—"

"Looks like we're done here?" Camden placed his warm arm around Iris's waist as he asked Zimmerman to let them go. "The kids are asleep in the car. Mrs. U is waiting."

Iris nodded. *Whoa. I'm losing it.* "I'm sorry, Detective. I'm just tired."

"Hey, we all are. Take it easy, and we'll talk soon." Zimmerman walked off before Iris could stop him again.

Iris followed Camden to her car, now parked behind Camden's pickup truck.

"How about you drive your own truck?" Iris asked.

"No. I don't think you should drive tonight. I'll get a ride back here tomorrow to get my truck."

"I don't want the children to come back to this house."

"I don't blame you."

"I need to get a job fast, Cam, and earn some income to rent a place for these kids until my sister comes home." She stopped outside her car. "Christmastown is seasonal. Temporary."

"No healthcare?"

"None. Pray for us?"

"I've been praying." Camden ran a finger over her chin. "I'll keep praying. I love you so much. I'm glad you're okay. Thank God."

"Yes, thank God."

Camden pecked her on the cheek. "Let's go."

As they got into the car, Iris replayed what Camden had said to her a few times now.

I love you so much.

This afternoon, he had made a similar statement.

I loved you then, Iris.

I love you now, and I will love you always.

Iris wondered if she could say the same thing to Camden. She had loved him once a long time ago.

Could she love him again?

As they left the blue and red lights in the distance on the rearview mirror, Iris felt tired. So tired.

"Iris?" Camden called her name.

She rolled her head slightly toward him. "I'm tired."

"I know, but this is important. Just want to ask you a couple of things about tonight."

Iris didn't know what he was going for, but his voice had an edge to it, as if he was a man on a protective mission.

It warmed her heart that Camden cared.

Still... "Can it wait until morning?"

"Tell me one thing, and we'll talk again in the morning."

Iris nodded.

Slowly, Camden paced out his words. "Tell me every word that Simon said to you."

CHAPTER TWENTY-FOUR

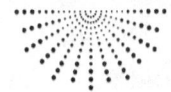

*C*amden didn't want to force Iris and the kids to return to the house of death, but Iris had no money to pay for a rental apartment. Her Christmastown job was now moot, as Mrs. Untermeyer's new business partner would be arriving in a week's time to take over the daily operations.

Yes, apparently people did prepare for Christmas as early as July.

He would bring his own office manager with him, thereby negating the need for Mrs. Untermeyer to hire Iris.

So Camden did what he had to do.

"Really? You want me to apply for that job?" Iris asked as Camden backed up his truck into Bianca's driveway.

It was sunny this morning. No rain. They could

load up quite a bit of the children's belongings. Mrs. Untermeyer had agreed to let Iris and the kids stay in her basement apartment that Camden was still renting.

In fact, the semiretired businesswoman had been so happy about the new arrangement that she offered to babysit the kids again this morning so that Camden and Iris could go back to Bianca's house to collect the children's toys and clothes.

Before they reached Bianca's house, Camden had broken the second piece of good news to Iris, but could see disbelief in her face.

"I'm disappointed you think so poorly of me," he said. "Surely you know better."

"I only wanted clarification." Iris climbed out of the truck, and stared at the boarded-up window and front door.

Camden had an idea what she was thinking. The event of the night before was still fresh in his own mind, the third-party information jarring. He could not begin to comprehend what Iris must have felt she had to do to protect those three kids from a shot-up gunman.

"We don't have to go inside." Camden followed Iris around the house.

"I need to get our things. That's why we're here."

They reached the backyard that Camden had

mowed on Monday. He waited as Iris unlocked the kitchen door.

"So. About this job at the gun shop," Iris said. "How many days a week?"

"As much as you want. Bryce wants to take his wife on a cruise," Camden said. "My brother would hire you on the spot, and you know it. He'll put our résumés side by side, and he'd pick you over me."

"Because I've been an office manager?"

"Because you won nationals several times, and I missed the mark." Camden had settled in his mind that some people were better sharpshooters than he could ever be.

"That was back in college. A long time ago."

"Doesn't matter. He might ask you to be a firearms instructor."

"I don't think I'll pick up another weapon."

"You did last night."

Iris shrugged. "To protect the children."

"Well, many people who want to learn to handle firearms are doing it to protect their families."

"Not all. Some do it for recreational sports. Like my dad."

Camden wanted to say something about Iris's dad, but he was distracted. The kitchen and house smelled as strange as ever. He tried to open the kitchen window over the sink.

"That window has been painted shut," Iris told him.

The only other windows were in the living room, and half of them were boarded up. Camden spotted the dark, irregular stain on the carpet. That must've been where the gunman had met his end.

Iris went down the hallway.

"Tell me what to pick up," Camden said.

"Put some toys from the playroom into a laundry basket. I know Mrs. U has toys from long ago, but I don't want the girls to break her antiques."

"They look like junk to me."

"Don't tell her that." Iris laughed as she disappeared into the baby's room.

Camden made a quick work of his toy collection. He had no idea what girls played with, so he grabbed anything that looked halfway pink. He placed the laundry basket in the hallway, then went to find Iris.

She was leaning against the baby's changing table, her face hidden in her palms. Her shoulders shook.

"Shhh..." Camden hugged her from behind, folding his arms across her tummy and resting his face against her hair. "Shhh..."

He waited for it to pass.

He knew that Iris had held it all in for the sake of the kids and in front of Mrs. Untermeyer. At some point, she would have to face it, deal with it, and move on.

It had been like that for him every time he came off a mission, an assignment, an operation. There was a debriefing, yes, but the decompression often took a while.

The pain would carry on for years to come.

He turned Iris around and let her bury her face into his shirt. His arms were like a cocoon around this love of his life, who was suffering something that only she could bear.

Correction. God would bear it for her if she would let Him.

Silently, Camden prayed for Iris.

No matter what happened to him, all he wanted was for Iris to be safe, secure, and satisfied.

Satisfied with what?

Correction. With whom. Christ in her is her hope of glory.

"Let it out, sweetheart." Camden stroked her back. Just like old times.

Eventually, Iris eased up. She sighed. "Life is hard."

"It could get harder once we find Bianca," Camden said.

Iris nodded.

"I'm sorry I can't sugarcoat that. God carries us through the hardships of reality."

Iris nodded again. "You know what's weird?"

"What, sweetheart?"

"Last night I wasn't afraid for myself. I didn't care what happened to me."

"You only wanted the kids to be safe. And they are. So we can thank God for that."

"God carried us through, Cam. The verse you reminded us of—Psalm 56:3—came alive last night. God was trustworthy and delivered us from danger."

"Well, good. To Him be the glory."

"Should I call Zimmerman and ask if he has made any progress?" Iris returned to her packing.

"I thought you called him this morning."

"And after lunch. He hasn't returned my calls."

"I'm not surprised." Before Iris could say anything, Camden quickly moved on. "What do you want me to carry to the car?"

"We'll need to bring all the diapers." She chuckled. "Then we'll need to get the girls' clothes and something for church on Sunday."

"I'm glad you're attending church with me, Iris."

"Me too."

"You could've decided to go to another church." Camden wished he hadn't said that. He didn't want to plant the idea that Iris could have gone elsewhere. He wanted her in his church.

If it's God's will.

And truly, it had to be God's will if they were ever to get back together again, memory kisses notwithstanding.

As his pastor friend Diego Flores had preached many times, one could not live in the present while being stuck in the past. The rearview mirror didn't look forward.

Well, forward isn't too bright right now.

Camden decided this was the wrong time to bring up the immediate future. That Homer art-theft case had adjourned to Europe. He had to leave on Friday for Frankfurt and then on to Brussels. He'd be gone a while.

He wondered how to tell Iris that.

She would probably be fine without him around, but he couldn't say the same for himself.

He knew now that he couldn't live without Iris.

Oblivious to his thoughts, Iris pointed to the box of diapers in a corner. "Could you take that to the car?"

The box had a lot of diapers in it, but it was lighter than it was bulky.

As Camden walked out of the baby's room and down the hallway, he heard two beeps coming from outside the house, indicating that someone had just locked a vehicle.

~

*S*ay it isn't so. *Two exes in the same place.*

Camden had forgotten his name, but not that fake chiseled face that could not be trusted.

The unwelcome visitor extended his hand. "Brock Owens. Remember me? We went to college together."

Whoopee. Camden had that giant box of diapers in both arms, and he wasn't about to put it down. Besides, he wasn't about to shake the hand of the guy who had moved with Iris to San Francisco eleven years ago.

Granted, it looked like their relationship hadn't lasted. *Well, good.*

What was he doing back in town?

"Can I help you?" Camden asked.

"I'm trying to recall your name. Camden, right? Camden La Salle."

"Yeah. What can I do for you?"

"I'm surprised to see you here. Is Iris around? Is she in the house? I need to talk to her."

Whoa.

Camden hadn't seen that coming.

Well, he hadn't thought that Iris might be in danger at all. There had been no indication of danger, even to the kids, until Monday night when the gunman had showed up.

Toxicologist reports would soon show what had

been in his system. And DNA tests would confirm —or deny—if he was Griffin's dad.

While there had been some evidence that Bianca had some goings-on, everything had suggested that she had strived to protect her children. Okay, except those possible visitors to the house.

Hmmm... In retrospect, Camden wondered if he should have insisted that Iris and the kids live somewhere else even from the day that Bianca had been reported missing.

Too late now.

It's truly by the mercy of God that they had been kept safe.

Camden stood rooted to the spot, holding the box of diapers, facing a ghost from Iris's past. "How did you know where Iris is?"

"Let me see her, and I'll explain."

Camden didn't move aside. To be sure, Brock could have walked around him. There was enough room for him to pass through between the dead hedges and the exterior wall of the house. "What's going on, Brock?"

"It's not your business—"

"Yes, it is. Anything to do with Iris is my business." It felt good for Camden to say that. He and Iris were heading somewhere good, and he wanted to preserve it. Had to preserve their relationship.

Right now, he felt threatened.

Brock smiled. "Ah, you two are back together."

"What do you want, Brock?"

"Iris has been on social media, asking for information. I have some. Let me talk to her."

"What information?"

"About Bianca."

CHAPTER TWENTY-FIVE

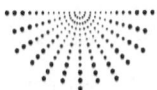

"**Y**ou and Bianca?" Iris hadn't expected it. Then again, she and Brock had broken up as soon as they both had moved to San Francisco.

Something that Camden probably didn't know.

It was then that Iris saw Camden staring at both of them. He was leaning against the exterior of the house, watching her talk with Brock. Behind him, the kitchen door was wide open. It looked dark inside compared to the bright afternoon sun.

"Seven years ago when I moved back to Savannah from DC, I ran for office," Brock Owens explained. "Bianca came to see me. She needed a job. I gave her a job shuffling papers and fliers for my campaign. I won, as you might know."

"I didn't know you ran for office, and I don't care that you did. All I want to know is one thing. Where's my sister?"

"I don't know where she is," Brock said. "I told Detective Zimmerman the same thing."

"He called you?"

"I called him when I heard the news last night that SWAT had killed a gunman holding the family hostage. I wouldn't have bothered, but when the reporter said three kids..." Brock cleared his throat. "Where's Peggy?"

Peggy?

"Sibley too?" Iris asked.

"I don't know about Sibley, but Peggy is mine."

In the sun, his golden hair reminded Iris of Peggy's hair. "I thought you got married to a lobbyist's daughter?"

Brock nodded. "We're celebrating our eighth anniversary."

"Peggy is five." Camden peeled himself off the wall.

"Yeah, nobody's perfect. I'm not going to get into details, but..."

"Let's do," Iris snapped. "My sister is missing, do you understand? She's been missing since last week. Did you know about it?"

"No, I didn't." Brock put up his hands in surrender. "Look, I talked to the SCMPD. I didn't have to come here. You didn't need to know that Peggy is mine. I didn't have to tell you anything. I came because..."

His voice trailed off.

It seemed to Iris that Brock had a great need to confess, to finally let someone know about some secret he had been keeping.

"Go ahead. We have all day," Iris said.

No, they didn't. They had to get back to the kids. The last thing Iris wanted was for Mrs. Untermeyer to get tired of the kids.

"I'm telling you, Iris, because I want you to know that I have nothing to do with Bianca's disappearance. In fact, I've done a lot for her the last six years. Do you have some water?"

"No. We came here to pick up some things. I can't stay in this house another night knowing someone died in it." Iris tried to remain strong.

"What's that about?" Brock asked. "Why are you here in Savannah in the first place? Did Bianca call you?"

"I ask the questions, Brock. So tell us. How did Peggy happen?"

Brock sighed. "Bianca worked at my campaign office, like I told you. My wife and I were bickering day and night, so she moved back to her mother's house in Charleston, and I pretty much lived at the office. Bianca kept me company. That was all."

"Stuff like that is never *all*, is it?" Camden asked.

"Speak for yourself. Look how you strung Iris along." Brock clenched his fists, as if wanting Camden to lunge at him.

Iris stepped in front of Camden, separating the two men. She could feel Camden breathing down her neck. She knew he was trying to keep a lid on it. She reached back with her hand and touched his arm.

Really, she wasn't trying to hold his arm back. She just wanted to touch him, to let him know implicitly that she was on his side. She rubbed his arm with her hand.

Slowly she felt his fingers interlock with hers.

Satisfied that Camden understood what she was trying to do, she turned her attention back to Brock. "How long were you and my sister together?"

"Not long. Just a year or so. We broke up because she was sleeping around."

"Oh, that's classic," Camden said. "You cheated on your wife with her, and then you dumped her because she was sleeping around."

"Don't judge me. You should never have let Iris go. Look in the mirror."

Camden squeezed Iris's hand. "Every day, man. Every day."

How could these men play nice at a time like this?

Iris cleared her throat. "So fast-forward five—six years. Did you pay for this house?"

Brock nodded. "Through various channels."

"Okay."

"And for multiple rehabs. She couldn't get clean. I'm tired of her asking for more money, I tell you. That boyfriend of hers—I don't want him near my daughter. But she said if I do anything about him, Renita would hear about us."

Iris leaned against Camden. His breathing and heartbeat were even, calm, quiet. Iris was confident that Camden no longer considered Brock a threat.

"I'm not running for office anymore. I'm going to retire and be the CEO of her father's company." Brock laughed. "If Renita and I are still married, that is. It's not looking good."

Neither Iris nor Camden laughed with him.

"I wanted Bianca to get back on her feet so she could be a proper mother to Peggy."

Proper. "How altruistic."

"I will only pay for child support if she's sober. I can't expect her to drive Peggy to kindergarten this fall if she can't see straight."

Iris braced herself. "When was the last time you talked to Bianca?"

"She called me three months ago. Drunk. Shot up. Said she was calling the TV station about us. I said I'll send her money if she checked into a rehab center."

"She did?"

"Only for thirty days. I haven't heard from her since," Brock said. "That's all I have for you."

This was not the time to tell Brock that he reaped what he had sown, but Peggy would remind him of that every day the rest of his life.

"If Bianca comes back, I'm not paying another dime." Brock lifted a finger. "You tell her that."

"I'm not your messenger. You tell her yourself."

Iris felt sad for her sister. It sounded like Bianca's substance abuse problem had gotten worse. She had sounded sober over the phone last Christmas, but then phone calls could be deceiving.

And that was seven months ago.

Anything could have happened between then and now.

"I have to go." Brock handed Iris a business card. "Yolanda's my attorney. Call her if Peggy needs anything. Her school starts early August, and she's fully funded through college."

"Wow. Through college?"

"Whatever you need, ask Yolanda. She'll take care of it."

"Did you see my posts on Facebook and Instagram last week?" Iris asked.

"I might have."

"But you didn't do anything about it. Bianca could be in danger!"

"I had nothing to say, but with the news reports of someone getting killed last night, I had to assure my wife that I had nothing to do with it." Brock sighed. "I fessed up this morning about Peggy. Renita's pitching a fit and talking to her attorney. I guess I could always get another wife."

Iris's jaw dropped. "Marriage is not a fish market."

"Whatever. Again, I'm sorry."

"Tell that to Peggy."

"As long as I know she's all right, it's all good."

Iris bristled. "Don't you think your daughter deserves better?"

"I'm giving her a fortune as it is. What more does she want?"

"A father's presence? Love?"

"I don't think I'm cut out to be anyone's father. I wasn't there when she was born. If not for the paternity test, I was almost sure she was someone else's."

It broke Iris's heart hearing that.

Peggy is an innocent child. It's not her fault that her parents messed up.

It made Iris more determined to do her best to help her sister's kids—all three of them. First, she had to get a job. Second, she had to—

Strike that.

First, I have to pray that God would have mercy on us all.

CHAPTER TWENTY-SIX

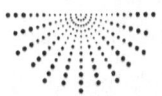

"*D*o you remember this spot?" Camden asked as they stopped at the edge of the riverfront, where a low concrete wall separated them from the Savannah River.

Around them, the warm evening breeze washed into the night. The sky was clear, and people were out and about. It wasn't too crowded this Thursday evening, but it was summer, and tourists were everywhere at all times of day and night.

Up the river, the Talmadge Memorial Bridge flickered with lights. Down the river, a noisy riverboat chugged its way on a cruise.

Camden was aware that this was a favorite hangout of friends from Riverside Chapel, but he had hoped that no one else was out on this Thursday night. He had timed it as best he could, eleven years to the date—off by a day or so—of that evening he had tried to forget, but couldn't.

That moment when he had thought, for sure, that Iris would say yes.

Instead, she had kissed him and run away across the country.

This evening, he was surprised that Iris had agreed to grab a quick bite at Piper's Place on River Street, just minutes from here. Sealing the deal had been Mrs. Untermeyer's willingness to watch the kids, read them the Bible before they went to bed, and tuck them in.

"Why did you bring me here?" Iris asked. "I agreed to soup and salad at Piper's, not a romantic stroll to nowhere."

Maybe this is a bad idea.

Camden dug his hand into his jeans pocket. Fiddled with the little box he had kept all these years.

He prayed for bravery. "You said you prayed for me, Iris."

Iris looked at him in a funny way. "You could tell me that on the drive back to Mrs. U's house."

"You prayed that God would give me confidence," Camden continued.

"I did."

"So hear me out as I practice being confident. Okay?"

Iris stood there. "Go on. I'm waiting."

Camden held Iris's hand and led her to the low wall. They sat down.

The wind blew through Iris's wavy brown hair, darker in the night, beckoning him to run his fingers through it

He cleared his throat. "Eleven years ago, I asked you a question. You didn't give me an answer."

"I transferred to another college."

Ah, so she does know what I'm talking about.

"If the family tragedy hadn't happened back when we were in college, would you have said yes?" Camden asked.

"I think I...yes."

"If I were to ask you the same question now, and there were no current family crisis, would you have said yes?"

"I can't right now. You said it yourself, Cam. I'm in the middle of a family crisis."

"But life is not always nice and clean. Life is complicated, complex, confusing." Camden's thumbs caressed the back of Iris's hands.

At least she didn't pull away.

"We're stronger together than apart, Iris. Aren't we two peas in a pod, like you said the other day?"

"I said we're *almost* like two peas in a pod."

"Close enough." Camden prayed before he spoke again. "With all my heart, I believe that God wants you and me to be together the rest of our lives."

"This is not a good time, Cam."

"When will a good time be?"

Iris shrugged. "Maybe never."

"If you think this is a bad time, then I submit to you that it's just as bad a time for us to be sitting here talking to each other when we should be sitting at home, wringing our hands and worrying about things outside our control."

Iris let go of Camden's hands. "Why the hurry?"

"You mean, we've waited eleven years, so what's a few more years?"

"Be serious."

"All right." Camden had to tell her. "I have to go out of the country tomorrow, and I don't want to lose you."

~

"Where are you going?" Iris searched Camden's face for clues regarding his real feelings for her.

Had he brought up their unfinished business from the past only before he had run out of time? Such things shouldn't be taken lightly.

What's going on, Cam?

She couldn't see much in the dim lights of the streetlamps.

"They tracked down the thieves..." Camden hesitated.

They were surrounded by people milling about, though the crowd seemed to be ignoring the couple sitting at the edge of Savannah.

"I don't need to know the details." Iris leaned into Camden's shirt, breathing in the smell of dryer sheets.

At once, eleven years folded like an accordion, and she was back in the previous Savannah, brimming with life and youth and all sorts of possibilities before her whole world collapsed on top of her like a heap of landfill.

She had done the only thing she knew to do: run.

Camden had been right.

Her indecision about him had caused her to take flight.

Camden kissed Iris on the top of her head.

"The assignment is overseas for five or six weeks," he said.

"That's not too long."

"If it works out, I might head up a joint office there in Europe somewhere."

"Oh."

"It could be years before I return. What if God calls me to be over there?"

"Is that a problem?"

"What if God doesn't call you to go?"

"Then it's a good thing we're not married to each other." Iris barely smiled.

"So we'll never see each other again."

"Cam, have some confidence in God, will you? He shall bring to pass what is good for us, in His timing."

Camden nodded. "Meanwhile, this project over there—I can't say where—is going to require me to be incommunicado for most of the five or six weeks. I won't know if you're all right. You won't know what's happening to me."

"When I'm afraid, I have to put my trust in God. Psalm 56:3." Iris knotted her eyebrows together. "I think you fear that I'll be gone when you come back to Savannah."

Iris saw tears pool in Camden's eyes. Or was it the reflection of the streetlamps around them?

"I fear that I will not return to Savannah," Camden said. "Just when you're back in town, I'm the one to leave. How ironic is that?"

"Trust God to keep us safe, Cam." Iris put her hands in Camden's warm grip.

Camden blinked. "I guess I was afraid that Brock would get to you before I do."

"Brock?" Iris laughed. "Don't worry. He doesn't hold a candle to you."

Camden's eyes brightened.

"So ask me again when you finish this assignment, okay? I hope that by then the SCMPD would've found Bianca, and life would get back to normal. We'll see where God leads us then."

"Will you miss me?" Camden stroked her arms.

Iris nodded. "Does it surprise you?"

"Well, I don't know."

"If I say I've missed you all these years, would you be upset I didn't decide one way or another to contact you?"

"You decided, all right. You decided *not* to contact me."

"I was still thinking about it." It wasn't much of a defense, but there it was.

"You're funny, Iris." Camden chuckled into her hair. "Your problem is more serious than I thought."

"My problem?"

"Indecisiveness."

Iris drew back and pretended to be annoyed. "And you? What of your lack of confidence?"

"I'll be more confident if I knew that"—Camden's voice dropped—"you'll be waiting for me."

"Do you need assurance?"

"Yes, I need a lot of assurance."

"Well..." Iris pulled Camden to his feet.

She drew his face toward hers, planting slow and gentle kisses on his cheek, chin, and then on his waiting lips.

"There," Iris said. "Feel assured now?"

"Not quite." Camden fingered Iris's lips. "I need something that will last six weeks..."

And his lips didn't let hers go until his iPhone buzzed repeatedly. Instead of answering it, he turned off his phone.

Then he resumed their parting kisses.

CHAPTER TWENTY-SEVEN

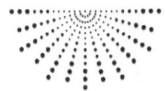

*T*here would be no sleep for him tonight.

Camden had misgivings about going to the butcher shop alone, but the witness said he would speak to him on his break if he brought a thousand dollars.

When Jerome Pendegrast had called—interrupting Camden's moment with Iris at the waterfront—he had left a voicemail that his community search team had received a name.

Camden had thought it seemed like a ridiculously high price to pay to talk to a night butcher for fifteen minutes. That was, until he called Ming. And Ming called Helen Hu. And Helen Hu called Detective O'Dell.

When O'Dell heard whom Camden was meeting, he rolled out the hundred dollar bills like they had been in his pockets all along.

It had turned out that the SCMPD, together with the FBI, had been trying to bust a coastal drug ring going up to Charleston, South Carolina, and down to Miami, Florida, and they were willing to put up the money.

Within an hour, Camden was driving a rental car to the Eckersall Butcher Shop in Port Wentworth, on the other side of Garden City, praying all the way that this new lead would pan out.

Jerome Pendegrast and Detective Zimmerman had been busy all week working on the same things from separate angles and perspectives, but it seemed that they had been running in circles.

Until now.

Passing around the photographs of Bianca Delaney in compromising positions had never been Camden's idea. It was all Jerome's. The man was desperate, as if paying a penance for losing his own adopted daughter. Granted, everyone believed that Jerome's daughter had run away from home, and one couldn't have stopped an eighteen-year-old from doing whatever she pleased.

Still, the photographs had done the trick.

Camden pulled into the back of the building in the thick of night, and there the guy was, smoking something.

The awfully thin man came to the car.

Leyshon, an alias.

"Lawton?" Camden asked. "Lawton Coffey?"

The man nodded. "Let's see it."

Camden pointed to the building. "Cameras."

"They're turned off."

Camden raised an eyebrow. "Yeah?"

"Yeah."

"Why?"

"A thousand reasons," Lawton said.

Camden lifted a black plastic bag just high enough to show that there were bills inside.

Lawton reached into the window.

"Not yet." Camden put the bag down. "Let's take a drive."

"I only have fifteen minutes."

"I'll bring you back in ten."

Camden drove around the blocks, letting Lawton count his bills. "Tell me about Simon Joe Flavell."

"We used to work in downtown Savannah together until he got fired."

"For?"

"Well, you know..."

"No, I don't know. Spell it out for me, Lawton. It's worth a thousand bucks."

"Doping. She got him into it."

"She?"

"That woman in the photos going around. Some hot chick. Slept with all of us."

"You too?"

Lawton looked away. "Stupid fool that I was."

Camden saw the emotional button. "We've all been fools, but she could be in danger."

"Do I look like I care?" Lawton laughed.

"She has three kids. No matter what she has done, the kids need her."

"Better no mother than a bad mother."

"What made you say that?"

"She and Simon. I don't think they'll ever come clean."

"Simon's dead," Camden said.

"Oh. I didn't know."

"The police are looking for Bianca." Camden asked God to forgive him for that bit of half-truth.

It was true that the SCMPD was looking for Bianca. It was also true that Simon was dead. One could connect the two facts in so many different ways.

Camden didn't want to spell it out for Lawton, and he also didn't want to explain that Simon had died at the hands of the SWAT team. It could influence Lawton away.

Then again, it gnawed at Camden, these bits of misleading statements.

How could he ask God to protect him in his sin?

Sin?

It's just a small little—

No.

Camden had been inured to lying—for a good cause—way back when he had been one of the more efficient FBI agents around. However, the last four years outside the system had been a time of retreat and introspection for him. He had taken this new job as a PI at Ming's company only because he needed the money.

But it was probably time to leave this type of business to someone else with a stronger fortitude. If he hadn't given the job at the gun shop to Iris, he would probably be a happy camper working as a straight-arrow store manager the rest of his life and never having to chase down perps like this one here.

"Buckle up," he told Lawton.

The man did it without complaining.

"You saw the news?" Camden asked, driving slowly on the empty street.

"I don't watch the news. I'm in a new job. I work the night shifts. I sleep all day long. End of story."

"You speak well."

"Did you expect me to use incomplete sentences?"

Whoa. For a butcher... Then again... "It was a compliment."

"Oh. Thank you. In fifth grade, I wanted to be a

poet." Lawton looked distressed, even under the streetlights.

"So be a poet."

"In high school, my stepbrother got me down the wrong path."

"You can still turn your life around. How old are you?"

"Twenty-two."

"You're still a kid. Go back to school, get a degree, be a poet."

"I still can't get the girl."

"What girl? Bianca?"

"I know, I know. She's thirty-six or seven." Lawton waved his arm. Black, smudgy tattoos up and down it. "But I like me a mature woman."

"I hear you." Camden tried not to think of Iris. It was too easy for his mind to go to her. Too hard for him to compartmentalize. He reminded himself that the FBI and SCMPD were listening in on this conversation.

The dashboard clock told him he was almost out of time.

"So you have a thing for Bianca." Camden decided to keep it in the present tense. Keep Lawton thinking there was still hope. "That's why you're talking to me."

"If I could get her back—nah. Simon has first dibs—oh, he's dead. Are you sure he's dead?"

"Like I said, didn't you watch the news?" Camden had to justify his earlier statements.

Misleading the witness!

He could hear the gavel now.

He could hear something else: Lawton's words. "You said you want Bianca back. Do you know where she is?"

"She's in a place no one can go."

"Is she alive?" Camden asked, almost too quickly.

Silence.

"You do know that I'm not the police," Camden added. "Just a family friend. Our *church* is trying to find Bianca to return her to her kids."

"Cute kids."

"Aren't they?" Camden waited to see if he should emphasize church one more time. "Our church is praying for Bianca."

It didn't resonate.

Camden tried again as he pulled into the butcher shop back parking lot. "It won't work against you, whatever you tell me. It might help Bianca and her kids. They need their mother."

Lawton thumbed the plastic bag on his lap.

"That money is yours." Camden stopped the car. "Why should you share it?"

"Yeah. Why should I?"

"It's a lot of money I just gave you. And all you

told me was that you're Bianca's ex. I already knew that. That's not enough information. I think you best return me the money."

Lawton tightened his grip on the bag.

"Give me something to justify the cash in that bag. Something to help Bianca's babies. They need their mother."

Lawton didn't get out of the rental car.

He only stared at the plastic bag. Finally, he turned to Camden.

"For another thousand, I'll tell you about the cabin in the woods."

CHAPTER TWENTY-EIGHT

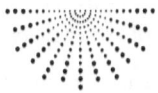

he cabin in the woods—where Lawton the butcher had written poetry about lost loves and missed opportunities—turned out to be an abandoned shack near the Ogeechee River between the city of Statesboro and the Georgia–South Carolina state line.

Lawton himself had refused to go there, citing the "stabbing wounds of misery" in his heart. Instead, he had handed Camden a printed copy of a poem he had written this year, an ode entitled "Bianca Delaney Who Could Never Be."

In turn, Camden had turned that over to Detective Zimmerman and somehow managed to get permission to accompany Zimmerman, his people, and representatives from the Georgia Bureau of Investigation to the edge of the search area.

But the road was as far as SCMPD, the GBI, and the FBI would let Camden go.

By then it was daybreak. Dawn arose into the Georgian sky, casting a pall over the landlocked greens of middle-of-nowhere Georgia.

From where Camden was standing outside his pickup truck, it seemed serene, peaceful. He could not hear the river. He could not see it.

All he could see were all-terrain vehicles, cadaver dogs with their handlers, and the ominous atmosphere of a massive search in the area, "where the river meandered into the lost night," the last line in Lawton's poem.

The landowner had said that the shack had been abandoned in the eighties. The roof had caved in, and there was hardly any shelter from the weather. He had wanted to sell the land, but nobody would buy it.

As Camden climbed back into his truck, mulling over what the landowner had said about a cabin that Camden had not been allowed to visit, he decided that he might as well return to Statesboro and have some breakfast.

He counted that he had roughly seven or eight hours left of Friday before he had to run to the airport and fly to Brussels to chase after the art thief.

He had tried and failed to reschedule this flight.

He had figured that if Ming could let him move his flight to Sunday afternoon, he could spend the morning with Iris and the kids at church before he had to leave for six weeks of constant traveling across Europe.

Ming had vetoed it. The European trail was getting cold.

Oh well.

Once in Europe, he could be done with the project in five weeks, but he had packed for six, just in case.

Helen Hu had not bought Ming's PI company, but she had been outsourcing a lot of work to them. She and Ming had discussed a joint office in Brussels or Frankfurt for their European operations.

With reluctance, Camden had been drawn into that conversation primarily because he was still single.

He had tried to change his status—again!—the night before, but he would have to admit he'd timed it poorly.

He glanced at his watch and prayed for Iris to have a good interview in a couple of hours. Then he added a quick prayer that God would keep him awake the rest of the day.

As he put his truck in reverse, he saw a van come down the road and slow down, decals of the local TV station emblazoned across every side. A cameraman and someone with a microphone disgorged from the news van.

Uh-oh.

I'd better warn Iris.

CHAPTER TWENTY-NINE

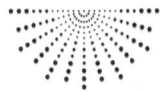

*I*ris arrived bright and early at the River Run Gun Shop at the edge of Savannah, dressed in a brand-new pair of hunter-green slacks and a matching floral blouse that she had bought at a Walmart—and changed in the women's restroom—on the way here.

It took Iris a while to get out of her car when she saw the River Run Indoor Range building behind the gun shop. The range had been where she and Dad had done target practices many years ago.

The painful memories made her want to put the car in gear and get out of there.

I don't need this job—

Yes, I do.

Well, she needed a paying job pronto. And the

job had to have some flexibility in it so that she could take care of Bianca's kids until she returned.

Mrs. Untermeyer—*bless her heart!*—had gone out of her way to accommodate three little kids in her house. But if Iris didn't start paying rent on the basement apartment soon, they would overstay their welcome and impose on Camden's pocket book.

The basement apartment had been leased to Camden in the first place. He had insisted on paying the rent for it until Iris got a job. Meanwhile, Camden had been sleeping in his older brother's guest bedroom.

Two blocks from here.

The dashboard clock told Iris she had better get into the shop before Bryce La Salle declared her late and incompetent.

She dragged herself out of the car.

Lord Jesus, if this is the job You want me to have, make it clear to me.

The sign on the door said that the shop opened at 10:00 a.m. While it was only 9:16 a.m. on Iris's watch, the door was unlocked.

Bryce greeted her at the checkout counter.

He looked like an older Camden.

Is this how Cam would look like in his fifties?

Iris wondered how it would feel to grow old with Camden, whether their kids would look anything like them at all.

She wondered what she would be doing at fifty. Camden would be fifty-four then.

Would God give them the gift of healthy years so they could enjoy each other?

They had lost so much—eleven years—and could never regain those years back, with time being linear and all.

Eleven years.

Gone.

But the next eleven, twenty, thirty years, were still ahead of them. Could she—should she—give Camden a go?

Lord Jesus, if Camden is the one for me, make it clear to me.

Bryce smiled. "Are you ready for the interview?"

Iris nodded.

Bryce motioned for one of his employees to take his place at the cash register. Then he led Iris through the gun shop.

Everything from the shelves to the flooring still looked the same as it had been eleven years ago. Iris knew exactly where everything was located.

"I was going to renovate this place, but my wife wants to go on a cruise," Bryce said. "Can't have everything."

"There's always next year."

"True." Bryce led her down a short hallway. At

the end of the hallway there were two ways to go. One led to the offices. One led out to the next building.

When Bryce chose the latter exit, Iris froze.

"We're going to the...range?"

He must've sensed the trepidation in her voice, because he stopped. "Yes, if you do well there, you have the job. I've already read your résumé from Tuesday. It's more than any of my employees here have achieved, except maybe for Nash and Greta, so... They're waiting for us."

Iris didn't know what to say.

I don't want to go there.

"In case you're wondering, the range looks nothing like what it was. We've renovated the entire building four years ago. You wouldn't even recognize it. I'll show you Cam's new favorite bay."

Cam.

Somehow his mentioning Camden eased Iris's heart. She didn't know why Camden had such an effect on her, as though he was meant to comfort her.

But would she let him?

216

CHAPTER THIRTY

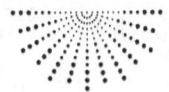

*C*amden waited as long he could before he went to see Iris at Mrs. Untermeyer's house. It would give time for more updates—if any—from Detective Zimmerman. When nothing had come, Camden had left Statesboro and headed back to Savannah.

He drove to his brother's house, showered, and napped for about an hour to clear the fog in his head. He ate some leftovers from the refrigerator before he went see Ming.

Ming gave him a hard time about the extra fees he had to pay to move his flight by several hours. And no, Ming refused to move it to any other day.

The art thieves had already moved the Homer artwork, and they were getting harder to track. Interpol agents on the ground were at their heels, but the thieves were still waiting for a buyer. If Ming's team didn't move quickly enough, the Winslow Homer national treasure would be lost forever.

Camden had to fly out tonight.

This is wearing me down.

I'm not cut out for this stuff anymore.

He needed a new career, a change of scenery. Unfortunately, he had given his only other job opportunity to Iris.

By the time Camden arrived at Mrs. Untermeyer's house, it was after lunch. Iris was on the porch talking on the phone, apparently with her landlord in Jacksonville.

Camden heard her repeating what the landlord had said on the phone—she had only one week to clear out her things from the apartment.

Camden couldn't imagine seeing Iris's stuff on the curbside. Unfortunately, he had to go out of the country and couldn't go with Iris to Jacksonville to move her things out of her apartment.

Before Camden could speak, Iris made another phone call. Camden was pleased that Iris had a wonderful women's Sunday school class, and somehow in the course of the next two minutes, five women volunteered at once to go with her on Saturday.

While he waited for Iris to get off the phone, he

peeked in the window and saw the kids playing in the living room on the other side of the wall. He went to the door to make sure it was shut tightly. He didn't want those three Delaney kids to hear what he had to say to Iris.

Iris was drinking soda from a can.

"What did my brother say?" Camden asked as he sat down on the Adirondack chairs. They were in the shade, but the weather still felt hot to him.

"You drove here to ask me that?"

"Well, preamble."

"You're funny." Iris placed the soda can on the side table. "He said he liked my résumé. We went to the shooting range to meet with a couple of people working for him."

"He didn't say he would give you the job?"

"I'll find out Monday. He said he is interviewing one more person."

"He said that? I don't think he has anyone else in mind but me."

Iris smiled. "Why did you let me have this, Cam? You're perfect for that establishment. You practically grew up there."

"You need a job. I already have one. Share and share alike."

"If I didn't know any better, I'd say you want me to stay in town."

Camden nodded. "That too. I'll be honest."

Iris crossed her legs. "Okay. So be honest with me now. You're supposed to be on a flight to who knows where right this minute."

"Brussels. It got moved to this evening."

"I don't sense an air of panic, so I know something is off."

Camden leaned back. "You read me well."

"I've always read you well. Out with it."

Camden let her wait. He prayed a bit, thought a bit, then prayed a bit more. "Do you remember last night when we were by the river?"

Iris nodded.

"Do you remember my phone ringing like crazy?" Camden asked.

"You turned the whole thing off."

"Yeah. Well, after I dropped you off, I checked my voicemail. It was Jerome."

"Yes?"

"They had a lead."

"A good one?"

Camden closed his eyes, nursing a headache from his lack of sleep. He couldn't drink any more coffee.

"Detective Zimmerman may or may not pay you a visit in the next few days, but I want to warn you ahead of time," he said slowly. "I don't want you to see this on the six o'clock news tonight."

Iris's face paled.

Camden's heart sank. This was the same porch they had kissed that Saturday evening. It held happy memories. Now he was going to offset that. He didn't know how to make it less painful than it could be.

Yet he had to be the one to prepare Iris.

No one else could do it.

He was the closest person to Iris now that her sister could possibly be...

"We don't know for sure all that's happening," Camden began. "We need to remember that God is with us."

"I know that."

"Monday night, you told me that Simon mentioned a man named Leyshon."

"Yes. I gave the same name to Detective Zimmerman." Iris sat up.

"Well, Zimmerman thought it was some guy who used to work at Eleanor's Pantry by the name of Leyshon Parnell. Fired for doping."

"But?"

"While Zimmerman went that route, I called in some favors." Camden didn't think it was necessary to tell Iris about his contacts at Fort Meade. "My friends crunched some data, cross-checked with Bianca's history and her supposed place of employment other than the grocery store, and came up with someone else."

Camden didn't say the name, and Iris didn't ask. Just as well that she didn't find out—now, anyway—that Lawton Coffey was a meat cutter at a butcher shop.

Who writes sorrowful poetry.

"Zimmerman couldn't do that research himself?"

"He's local. He doesn't have the contacts I do." The same contacts he had established back when he had been involved in national security. But again, Iris didn't need to know that. It would only make her worry.

Just as she'd be totally worried if she found out that chasing art thieves was not the only thing he was supposed to do in Brussels this weekend.

"When did you have that information?" Iris asked.

"Wednesday."

"And you waited until today to tell me?"

"It could be a dead end." He cringed at the word. He hadn't meant to say it. "I don't want to get your hopes up or down."

"It's not a dead end now, is it?"

"Last night, we set up a meeting. I went because this guy probably has been following the case in the news and knows the faces in the SCMPD. He doesn't know me. To him, I'm a concerned friend of the family."

"Tell me Zimmerman is involved."

"Yes. In fact, he and O'Dell are in charge."

"I don't know who that is."

"He's another detective at the SCMPD. But the point is, that's how the search outside Statesboro began."

Iris slid to the edge of her chair. "A search?"

"It could be nothing. I wanted you to know they're searching out there. I don't want you to see it on the six o'clock news while I'm out of town."

"Thank you for preparing me, but there's something you're not saying."

Camden wondered what Iris was getting at.

"What have they found so far?" Iris asked.

"Zimmerman won't tell me, and to be clear, I wasn't allowed inside the search perimeter, but Ming's contacts in the local area said they've been... uh, digging."

Camden studied Iris's face.

Iris nodded slowly, slowly.

Then she buried her face in her palms and lost it altogether.

CHAPTER THIRTY-ONE

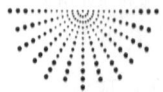

The whole scene replayed itself over and over in Camden's mind as he closed his eyes and leaned back against the headrest some thirty-thousand feet over the Atlantic Ocean that evening.

The memory of Iris losing her cool after he had mentioned the word *digging* had dug into his heart. His repeated assurance that God was in control hadn't stopped Iris from weeping.

Sometimes it was good to get it all out, though Camden had assured her that it was premature.

Perhaps it hadn't been just the potential breaking news that had affected her so.

Camden wondered how many times Iris had grieved over the past eleven years. It bothered him that he hadn't been with her to comfort her during those seasons of despair.

Despair?

Iris believed in Jesus.

There is no despair in Jesus.

There's always hope in Jesus, and Iris knows that.

Still, Camden had stayed with her until it was time for him to drive to the airport to catch his flight.

He was glad that Iris had recovered after realizing that there had been nothing definitive coming out of the search in the woods around the Ogeechee River.

The practical person that Iris was, she understood that she had to wait for Detective Zimmerman.

Camden couldn't tell her not to watch the news or get on social media to hear reports. He hadn't needed to remind her that the local news stations all tweeted live news.

All Camden had done was to remind Iris that God was sovereign.

And then Iris had surprised him when she told him to leave for the airport.

"Go to work, Cam. If you stay, you'll be in the way." Those had been her exact words.

Camden recalled his own shock.

"If you stay, I will look to *you* for support. Wouldn't it be better if I depend on God instead?"

"God brings family and friends to us in our times of need, Iris. I want to be a part of His support structure for you and the children."

"You already are, Cam. Now go. Get on that plane!"

CHAPTER THIRTY-TWO

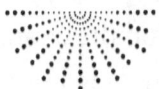

*W*hen Iris heard the door chime and saw Detective Zimmerman and Officer Garcia walk through the front entrance of the River Run Gun Shop, she knew.

She just knew.

She had been helping a customer choose a scope for his hunting rifle, when she had a gnawing feeling this afternoon would be more than just overcast and rainy.

She had been thinking of Camden, who hadn't contacted her since Friday, and of Bianca, who had been missing for over sixteen days.

She had been afraid to call Zimmerman to ask what was happening. Afraid of what the detective might say, afraid of bad news.

Whenever I am afraid,
  I will trust in You.

She was still reciting Psalm 56:3 to herself when she sent the customer to the checkout. Bryce was there and could ring up this purchase.

She waited behind the counter for Bryce to send Zimmerman and Garcia her way.

But when Bryce himself walked with them to her, she had no doubt in her mind what they were going to say to her.

"Is there someplace we can talk?" Zimmerman asked.

"My office," Bryce said. "This way."

Iris was right behind Zimmerman. His shoulders slouched more and more as they walked down the hallway, as if he were walking the plank off a tall ship. Iris wondered how many times the police officer had to break bad news to family members.

She tried to keep it together. After all, she had been grieving since Friday, even as she had sent Camden back to work.

Now she wished Camden were with her.

Yes, I'd like you to hold my hand and tell me everything is going to be all right.

Suddenly, Iris realized that the statement she had just made in her mind should have been directed to almighty God instead.

Lord Jesus, forgive me for my pride. Please hold me and tell me everything is going to be all right.

Walking beside her, Officer Garcia kept up with Iris's pace.

The entire entourage continued their funereal march to Bryce's corner office. It was a cluttered mess—a mini landfill—and Iris felt a sudden urge to clean up the place.

They all sat down on available chairs, with Bryce sitting at the edge of his metal desk.

Iris listened as much as she could, processing every other word, as Detective Zimmerman tried to give it to her in civilian lingo. Somewhere in there, she had managed to ask a question, though as soon as she had spoken, she had forgotten what she had asked.

"Yes, we think about two weeks, maybe two and a half," Zimmerman said. "It rained some, but the temperature out there was in the low nineties, even in the shade."

"Did you say my sister was buried in a shallow grave?" Iris's voice broke. The indignity of it.

Zimmerman nodded.

"Are you sure it's her?" *Did I mishear something?*

"There was too much skin fragmentation for us to take fingerprints, but her dentist provided us with the dental records, and there is no doubt."

"How did you know her dentist—oh yes, you have her bills and receipts from her house?"

"Yes, ma'am. It took three days for our forensic dentist to match the films, but it's fortunate that the Coastal Regional Crime Lab wasn't busy Monday."

"You found my sister's body Saturday night." That much she had heard.

And Bianca remained in the morgue on Sunday. *Sunday. A day of rest. A day of the Lord.*

"Yes, usually the crime lab is not open on weekends, unless it's a high-profile case."

"My sister is not." Iris wiped tears off her cheek with her fingers.

"Every person is important to us," Zimmerman said as Officer Garcia handed Iris a tissue paper from a box nearby.

"Thank you." Iris blew her nose. "You're not going to do more tests to make sure it's really Bianca? Like DNA? I gave you her toothbrush."

"It's a positive ID, ma'am. Her dental records match. No DNA tests are needed."

"I'm assuming you brought that guy in for questioning."

"Which guy, ma'am?"

"The one you thought was Leyshon somebody but turned out to be someone else." Iris remembered her conversation with Camden on Friday.

Camden.

Did he know? How could she tell him about this news? Could she get to him through his boss, Ming Wei?

"He's in custody. We're investigating all angles," Zimmerman said. "Don't worry. We got it."

"When can we have Bianca back to bury her?" Iris asked.

"The medical examiners have finished their work, so if you can get a funeral home to do some coordination, your sister will be released to you."

Bryce put up his hand. "I'll take care of it, Iris. I've lived here long enough to know the local businesses."

Iris nodded. "Thank you."

Turning to Zimmerman, Iris had more questions. "Bianca's ex, Simon, who came to the house, looked like he was on drugs."

Zimmerman didn't reply.

"My sister, as you know, had substance abuse problems in the past and had been in and out of rehab. Were drugs involved?"

She waited for Zimmerman to decide whether he was going to tell her or not. "You know, I'll hear it on the news anyway."

"They're not going to have any information," Zimmerman said. "Well, apart from the fact that we've been investigating a drug ring in the area for the last nine or ten months."

"So my sister could've been a victim."

"That, I can't tell you at this time. The toxi-cology report won't be available for another two—maybe three—weeks. We will find out the cause of death then. I'll let you know, ma'am."

That seemed to be the end of it for Zimmerman today, but not for Iris.

Where do I sign up? I want to put those perps away.

Iris decided to hold that thought in check. The last thing she needed to do right now was to make snap decisions based on emotions.

She had to think of the children.

Poor Peggy, Sibley—

Griffin.

Poor, poor baby.

He would grow up never truly knowing his birth mother.

CHAPTER THIRTY-THREE

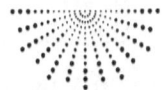

"*B*itter the night may be, but hopeful is the day of the Lord." Pastor Diego Flores's voice resonated across the casket over the freshly dug gravesite.

Iris dabbed her eyes as she held Griffin in her arms and lap. He had refused to be held by anyone else but Iris, and so be it. She had fed him and changed him before they arrived at this pristine cemetery in Savannah.

Somewhere to the east of this site, Mom rested.

Iris wept as quietly as she could, tears dripping down on Griffin's sailor outfit. The baby looked okay for now, but he was probably going to get warm soon.

Already, Peggy was fidgeting as she sat on her own folding chair next to Iris—with her new yellow purse with new and bigger smiley stickers all over it. Her navy-blue dress looked warm. It was a wool blend fabric, but Peggy had insisted on wearing it because it had been her mommy's favorite color, or so she said.

Five days after Detective Zimmerman had brought the bad news that Bianca had passed away, they had come here to bury her at the humid end of July.

The toxicology report had not been published, but for all practical purposes, there was nothing more to be done for Bianca.

Her life had ended at thirty-seven.

In a couple of hours from now, the weather would be midday hot, and they would all go back to their lives in a new normal.

For now, the rain in the night had subsided in the serene burial grounds, and the morning birds started to chirp around Pastor Flores's sermonette.

"The joy of the Lord is our strength," he continued. "Never forget that."

Iris was confident that the young thirty-something pastor of Riverside Chapel would not go on and on, as many people had to go back to work.

Many?

Not many people had shown up today, because it was a Monday, a workday. Still, she could see that at least twenty-odd people had indeed taken time off to come here, some from work, such as her new friends from church, Tina MacFarland and Priyanka Patel, both of whom were in the women's Sunday school class that Iris had started attending since she arrived in Savannah.

Tina and Priyanka had been kind to Iris since she had first met them at Riverside Chapel. Both had recruited church men to drive to Jacksonville to help Iris move her furniture out of her rental apartment a week ago.

And then there was Piper Peyton, who had donated all the food they were going to have for lunch at her restaurant, Piper's Place, after the graveside service. She was sitting on the other side of Mrs. Untermeyer, who was holding a sleepy Sibley on her lap.

Piper was staring at Heidi Wei-Flores on the other side of the casket. The pastor's wife was standing next to her husband, interpreting the sermon in sign language for Piper's benefit.

"God is good. God always encourages," Pastor Flores continued. "God walks with us through both expected and unexpected difficult times on earth."

Eventually, it was time for Iris to place a single rose on top of Bianca's casket.

Long ago, when Iris had been a teenager, Bianca had visited the family home. It had been the only time they had conversed in a sisterly way, as far as

Iris could remember. Somewhere in that conversation, Bianca had said that her favorite flower was the rose.

Roses had thorns.

A couple of tugs at Iris's black dress made her look down.

"Auntie Ibis," Peggy said, swinging her yellow smiley purse. "Why is Mr. Cam not here?"

Iris led Peggy back to their seat before she answered. "Mr. Cam has to work."

Somewhere in Europe, where he could not even text or email her. Iris wondered sometimes about that serious business of art theft and whether Camden did more out there than he could tell her.

"He doesn't get to say goodbye to Mommy," Peggy added.

So she understands what's going on here.

Iris could barely respond.

Peggy placed her two small hands on Iris's face. Her palms were still sticky and somehow smelled of peanut butter. Iris made a mental note to check Peggy's purse for the contraband.

"Please don't be sad, Auntie Ibis." Peggy's voice had a dulcet twang to it, like she was a proper southern lady.

Iris didn't know whether she had taken after Bianca or whether she had been mimicking Mrs.

Untermeyer. Still, she was at such an impression-able age.

Iris felt attached to these motherless children, and she was now suddenly worried. Could an aunt have legal custody of these kids if their fathers were still around?

Lord Jesus, please don't let their fathers separate these three kids. Please keep them together.

She could talk to Brock Owens and see whether he would let Iris be Peggy's guardian, but no one knew who Sibley's dad was. Griffin's dad was deceased, if Simon Flavell had been his true biolog-ical father.

Iris made another mental note to ask attorneys at church regarding such legal matters that she had not encountered before. If she were the legal guardian of these kids, she could ask for their birth certificates.

Then she realized what could be required of her.

Lord Jesus, if You want me to raise these children for Bianca, I will.

CHAPTER THIRTY-FOUR

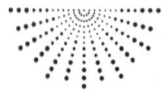

*I*ris had spoken to Brock Owens's family attorney in the days after the funeral. The attorney had mailed Iris a signed document saying that Brock would not contest her desire to be Peggy's legal guardian as long as he had visitation rights as the biological father.

As of today, one week after Bianca's funeral, Iris was still waiting for the court to approve her as the children's legal guardian.

Brock had agreed to take a paternity test to see if Sibley was also his, and everyone was anxious for the results that could take months. As for Griffin, Simon's parents were deceased, and no one in his family wanted him.

Well, I do!

To be sure, she wasn't waiting idly. Bryce had

worked her hard at the gun shop. While she had flexible hours where she could drop off and pick up Peggy and Sibley from school, it was still a task juggling all these sudden responsibilities that Iris hadn't known she'd have two months ago.

Today, for example.

Iris had to get Peggy to her first day in kindergarten.

Alone.

The verse from Psalm 56:3 played over and over in her mind as she shampooed Peggy's hair, washed it, dried it, and ushered the girl to the kitchen table, where she immediately spilled cereal on her uniform.

Iris wrung out a dishcloth and tried to wipe the milk as best she could, and then they headed upstairs, where Mrs. Untermeyer was waiting for Griffin and Sibley with open arms.

Sibley's preschool would start in two weeks' time. Iris had written it all down—somewhere.

By the time she buckled Peggy into the booster seat, Iris was sure she had forgotten something. She prayed they didn't have to turn back to the house once they got into Savannah traffic.

Mrs. Untermeyer's house was fifteen minutes away from the private Christian school that Brock had paid for Peggy to attend, but traffic stretched that to forty minutes.

God is all I need.

God is my strength and song.

Iris found a parking spot, and in no time at all, she and Peggy were heading to the front entrance of the brightly colored—almost psychedelic—kindergarten. Every little kid around them was dressed in the cutest primary color outfits of his or her choice.

Peggy was dressed all in bright yellow, from top to skirt to socks to backpack.

Iris had made her leave her smiley purse in the car, having reminded her that she could lose it in the big building.

When it was time for Peggy to go, Iris couldn't let go of her hand.

Peggy tugged. "Auntie Ibis?"

Iris wasn't sure if she wanted Peggy there at the twenty-thousand-dollar-a-year kindergarten. What could she learn there that Iris couldn't teach Peggy at home?

"Auntie Ibis?"

Iris knelt down in front of Peggy. She couldn't say a word.

"Are you going to be okay, Auntie Ibis?" Peggy asked.

Slowly, Iris nodded.

"God takes good care of us." Peggy patted Iris's shoulder.

Out of the mouth of babes...

Iris sniffled and stood up. She waved goodbye to Peggy as the girl walked with her head held high. She stopped suddenly and turned and ran back to Iris.

"I love you, Auntie Ibis!" Peggy hugged her tightly.

"I love her too!" a male voice said somewhere behind Iris.

Iris spun around. Her jaw dropped.

"Mr. Cam! Mr. Cam!" Peggy jumped up and down. She ran toward Camden, and he swept her up in his arms.

"First day of school, huh?" Camden asked.

Peggy nodded her head vigorously. Then she leaned toward Camden's ear and whispered something.

Iris frowned.

"You can let me down now, Mr. Cam." Peggy wiggled. "I have to go to school."

"Well, okay." Camden put her down, and Peggy ran to the front entrance where a greeter met her.

Before Iris realized what was happening, Camden had slipped his arms around her waist. She leaned back against his chest.

"She's growing up fast," he said quietly.

Iris could feel his breath on her neck. She waved to Peggy, disappearing into the building.

Camden turned Iris around.

She noticed that he had let his hair grow out a bit, and he had a five o'clock shadow on his chin. He looked like he hadn't gotten much sleep.

"Happy to see me?" Camden asked.

Iris nodded. Her lips quivered.

"Where are you parked?"

Iris pointed.

"Are you letting me do all the talking?" Camden planted a kiss on the top of her forehead.

Iris pulled away slightly to dig for some tissue paper in her jeans pockets. She found a crumpled piece that could have been a few days old. She wiped her nose with it.

"I'm sorry I missed the funeral." Camden held her hand as she led him to her car. "By the time I found out, it was Wednesday."

"Don't worry about it. You hardly knew Bianca."

"I know you, and I wish I'd been there to support you."

"You're here now. Do you have to leave again?"

"Nope. I'm back in town for the foreseeable future. We finished the job super early—two weeks —instead of the projected five or six, and we're done."

Iris stood at her car door. "So what are you doing next?"

"Ming's giving me another job, but I'm praying

about it." Camden fingered Iris's hair. "You used to have short haircuts. I didn't realize how wavy your hair is when it's long."

"It's the humidity." Iris brushed it off. "How did you know we'll be here at this time? Did you talk to Mrs. Untermeyer?"

"Two nights ago, actually. I told her not to say anything, because I wasn't sure if I could get a flight out."

Iris nodded. "The kids and I missed you."

"I missed you too. How are you holding up?"

"I have good days and bad days," Iris confessed. "Mainly, I'm trying to be strong for the kids."

"The joy of the Lord is our strength."

"Nehemiah. Glad you know your Scripture, Cam."

"I've been reading my Bible a lot while I was away. Praying about many things. Praying about us."

Iris looked into those eyes, bluer than ever in the Savannah morning sun.

"Speaking of kids, what did Peggy whisper in your ear?" Iris asked.

"You're a curious one."

"Tell me."

"Soon. I know you have to go to work now, but how about dinner tonight? I'll get a takeout and bring it over to your place." Camden rubbed Iris's arms. Her back was against her car.

"We'll ask Mrs. Untermeyer to join us."

"Anything you want, sweetheart." Camden leaned toward Iris.

And resumed his kiss from that Thursday evening at the riverfront weeks before.

CHAPTER THIRTY-FIVE

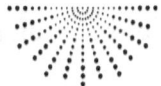

*I*ris stepped over sleeping cats on the outdoor rug as she carried the laundry basket through the screened-in covered porch.

Above her, the fan whirred. It was a pretty Saturday morning in September, just after Camden had driven over from his apartment two blocks away to have breakfast with her and the kids.

Of course, it was handy to have another adult help clean up the mess that Griffin usually made on his high chair. Iris had been impressed that Camden didn't mind getting his hands—and sometimes shirt —dirty while handling Griffin and his smashed baby food.

Camden finished folding Griffin's onesies and reached for the laundry basket in Iris's arms. He placed it on the floor next to his rattan chair as Iris sat down on the other chair at this corner of the porch outside the basement of Mrs. Untermeyer's house.

Iris had spoken with Mrs. Untermeyer the night before. Her oldest brother was still in the hospital in Atlanta, and she had decided to stay there for a few more days. They were running some tests to see why he had chest pains.

Iris had told Mrs. Untermeyer that she and the kids would pray for her family.

And they had, at breakfast this morning.

From her seat, Iris watched Peggy and Sibley crawl in and out of their play tent that someone at church had given to them. They were saying *peek-aboo* as they rolled in laughter.

When Iris picked up one of Sibley's tee shirts from the basket to fold, she noticed that Camden was staring at her. "What?"

"Nothing."

The laughter from the tent stopped.

"Auntie Ibis?" Peggy's head peeked out of the pink-striped tent.

"Yes, Peggy?" Iris folded more onesies.

"Can we have PBJ for lunch and dinner?"

"Sure. But vegetables are good for you too." Iris smiled. "It just so happens we have broccoli and kale."

"Ewwwww!" Peggy disappeared into the tent,

only to stick her head out one more time. "Mr. Cam?"

"Yes, Peggy?" Camden said.

"Will you marry us and make us PBJ every day?"

Camden glanced at Iris.

"This is a test, Cam." Iris waited to see what he was going to say.

Peanut butter and jelly sandwiches were only Peggy's new favorite food since the school year had begun.

Peggy crawled out of the tent and stood on her bare feet. "If you marry us, I promise to scoop the cat litter every week."

"Every week?" Camden raised his eyebrows. "Not every day?"

"Well, we can discuss options."

Discuss options?

By now Iris couldn't contain it anymore. She laughed so hard she had tears in her eyes.

"Where in the world did you learn to speak like that, Peggy?" Camden asked.

"At the kiddie garden." Peggy put out her hand. "Deal?"

"Hmmm..." Camden seemed to be pretending to consider Peggy's offer. "How about I marry your aunt instead?"

Iris stopped laughing.

"Not Auntie Ibis," Peggy said. "She's too sad."

"Sad?" Camden placed his hand on Iris's.

His palm felt warm to the touch. When Camden gave her hand a light squeeze, his warmth spread to her heart.

"Don't be sad, Ibis—I mean, Iris."

Iris said nothing and didn't look at Camden. It had been almost two months since Bianca had passed away, leaving her with three kids to tend.

The toxicology report had been published in the middle of August, and it was rather sad for everyone to hear—even Jerome Pendegrast, who had helped organize the community search teams—that Bianca Delaney had indeed died of a drug overdose. Investigations were pending into Lawton Coffey's involvement in the illegal dumping of her body.

Iris wished that her sister was still here so she could see that Griffin was crawling these days, and slowly trying to stand up, and that he had looked cute five minutes ago when Iris checked on him, having fallen asleep in the playpen just inside porch door.

Sleeping like a baby totally applied to Griffin.

"God is sovereign," Camden said. "God allows what He allows, gives what He gives, and takes what He takes. Blessed be the name of the Lord."

"Job 1:21," Iris said.

Naked I came from my mother's womb,
And naked shall I return there.
The Lord gave, and the Lord has taken away;
Blessed be the name of the Lord.

"Ah, you do know your Scripture." Camden sighed. "God works out all things for our good. Romans 8:28. And nothing separates us from the love of God."

"That's from Romans 8:38-39. Good reminders, Cam."

For I am persuaded that neither death nor life, nor angels nor principalities nor powers, nor things present nor things to come, nor height nor depth, nor any other created thing, shall be able to sepa-rate us from the love of God which is in Christ Jesus our Lord.

"Shall I go on?"

"No need. That's plenty."

Camden cleared his throat. "Iris Amelia Delaney, I've never stopped loving you. I love you always. Will you marry me? Be my wife and the mother of my babies?"

"Mr. Cam!" Peggy stepped forward. "You didn't say please."

"Uh, please?" Camden laughed.

"And kneel." Peggy pointed to the rug.

"What?"

"If you don't kneel, it's non-effect."

"It's what?" Camden's jaw dropped.

"Did you mean non-effective, perhaps?" Iris spoke up. "Peggy, who taught you that word?"

"Max says *non-effect* all the time." Peggy placed her hands on her little waist.

"Max who?" Iris was alarmed now.

"My boyfriend at the kiddie garden."

Iris gasped. "You can't have a boyfriend. You're not even six years old!"

Camden agreed. "You're going to have to wait until you're twenty-one, young lady."

"But I like him," Peggy said. "His daddy is a Tony. Auntie Ibis, what's a Tony?"

Iris frowned. "Attorney?"

Peggy nodded her head. "We said *non-effect* all week last week. Next week, Max is going to teach us a new word."

Oh dear.

Peggy turned to Camden. "Mr. Cam, I want to go back into my tent now. Are you going to kneel or not?"

So he did.

"Iris, I've loved you always. I've never stopped loving you." Camden held both of Iris's hands as she sat there blinking away the sting in her eyes.

"Even after we broke up so many years ago, I have truly loved only you. I tried to love other women, but no one had ever come close to you. Each was a poor substitute for the love of my life." He scooted on his knees to get closer. "Please marry me?"

Iris closed her eyes, nodded.

And felt Camden touch her left hand. She opened her eyes to find a pretty diamond ring sliding onto her ring finger. "Oh..."

"You like it?" Camden asked.

Iris nodded. "You came prepared."

"Been carrying this in my pocket since Zurich."

"I thought you were in Brussels."

"I was everywhere, chasing thieves." Camden gently pulled Iris to her feet. "I had an old ring, the one I almost gave you years ago. Then I realized that God is making all things new. I needed a new ring."

"It fits," Iris said.

"Of course. Your ring finger is the size of my left pinky." Camden looked like he's proud of his keen power of observation.

"Seriously?" Iris lifted her fingers in the sunlight. The ring sparkled.

And so did her love for Camden. Rekindled. Revitalized.

She was still smiling when Camden gathered her into his enveloping arms, sealing his promise with a kiss on her lips, the whole conclusion to his successful proposal cut short when Iris heard a wail in the background.

There was Griffin in his playpen, standing up on his chubby legs and grinning from ear to ear and saying, "Da-da! Da-da!"

CHAPTER THIRTY-SIX

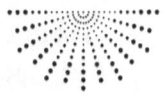

*C*amden's misgivings about the six-week-long premarital counseling at Riverside Chapel faded when he began to enjoy attending the couple's Bible study on lifelong marriages that Pastor Flores's father taught.

There were things he hadn't known about Iris that had come up in those sessions, things like how devoted she had been to the children's welfare.

"What if they eat cat food again?" Iris had asked during one of their carpools to the sessions.

"A little bit is not going to hurt them," Camden had said casually before he realized that was a no-no.

"I can't believe you said that!"

Stuff like that as they got to know each other.

And then there was that solemn drive to

Reidsville to visit Iris's dad at the state penitentiary. Iris had wanted to go alone, but Camden had reminded her that they were in this relationship together. It meant they had to weather tough times together. Go places together. Do things together.

Stuff like that.

The premarital counseling went from mid-September to the end of October. Fortunately, the church calendar had a free Saturday morning in early November for their wedding. That way, they could drive to New Smyrna Beach, Florida, that afternoon, stay overnight, and the next day drive an hour south to Port Canaveral, where a ship would be waiting to take them on a four-night cruise to the Bahamas.

But first, the wedding.

Ah, the wedding.

Camden was amazed that the wedding had cost more than the six weeks of premarital counseling. The photography, flowers, rehearsal dinner, reception, catering, whatnots, all added up to a pretty penny. He would never have dreamed of asking Iris to elope with him, but he had come close several times during their budgeting process.

Still, none of the expenses and long waits could compare to the pain of having to leave Peggy, Sibley, and Griffin behind. They would be in the good of hands of Mrs. Untermeyer and Camden's brother, Bryce, and his wife, but still...

Even Camden had shed a tear after the wedding and reception when he and Iris climbed into her car to drive south to Florida.

He had wanted to take her to the French Riviera. She had said it would be too far away from the children. They had compromised and agreed to go on a cruise to the Bahamas.

Camden looked forward to arriving in Nassau. He wanted Iris to meet his friends at the Chapel by the Sea, an old church that his friend, Byron Moss, attended. Camden had gone on a mission trip there about five years ago and they had hit it off.

Now he didn't want to leave Savannah either.

"You think the kids will be okay?" Camden asked as Iris turned onto the exit toward New Smyrna Beach three and a half hours after their wedding reception. They had taken turns to drive, and Camden had driven the first two hours.

"Ha." Iris replied. "What did I tell you, Cam? You miss them too."

The GPS led Iris to the oceanfront condominium complex they would be staying in overnight before they boarded the cruise ship on Sunday afternoon.

They had planned on either visiting a local

church for Sunday morning service, or watch River-side Chapel service streamed online.

"Too bad we're only staying here one night," Camden said after they had checked in and rolled their overnight suitcase to the elevator.

On the top floor, Camden swiped the key card in the door, and they entered the suite, greeted by a magnificent view of the Atlantic Ocean through a wall of glass.

Iris went outside to the balcony and stood at the railing, the wind blowing about her hair and dress.

Camden read the weather forecast on his iPhone on the way to join Iris. "It's seventy-seven degrees out."

"A whole fifteen degrees warmer than Savannah. Good idea to come here," Iris said as Camden kissed her neck and shoulders, the afternoon sun warming his face.

"I've been waiting for you for eleven years."

"You keep saying that, but it's almost twelve years now."

"Is it, really?" Camden could be a patient man, but now his time had come.

He wanted to be with Iris every day for the rest of his life. He didn't want to take up another project with Savannah River Investigations that required him to go overseas or travel anywhere.

"Do we really think that the kids are in good hands while we're gone for four nights?" Iris asked.

"Yeah, I think we'll be in trouble when we get back on Thursday. Mrs. U is probably spoiling them rotten as we speak—with all her holiday cooking and baking—and we'll have to deal with the fallout."

Iris giggled.

"If it were up to me, we'd be gone two weeks, but like you said, we could go somewhere on our first anniversary next year, when Griffin would be two years old and would do better with a sitter."

"Two weeks? What are we going to do for two weeks?"

"Oh, I have some ideas..." Camden caressed Iris's lips with his.

"Cam!"

"What? I meant sightseeing. Eating out. Stuff like that."

"Right."

"You have something else in mind?"

"I can think of a few things." Iris smiled.

Camden gathered her in his arms. "I love you, Mrs. La Salle."

"I love you too, Mr. La Salle."

"Always."

"Yes, always."

∽

DEAR READER:

I hope you enjoyed the love story of Iris and Camden in *Love You Always*. The next novel in the Savannah Sweethearts series is *Kiss You Now*, the story of Hunter Jacobs and Priyanka Patel. Hunter is a novelist suffering from writer's block and Priyanka is an ER doctor who is unable to practice due to a past trauma. Doing anything but the careers they have trained for, these two people meet on Tybee Island at the crossroads of their lives.

Kiss You Now
JanThompson.com/kiss

NEW TO SAVANNAH SWEETHEARTS?

Are you new to the Savannah Sweethearts series? Read the first novel for free! *Ask You Later* kicks off this series of clean and wholesome contemporary Christian romances set in Savannah and on Tybee Island by the Atlantic Ocean.

Ask You Later
JanThompson.com/ask-free

JOIN MY BOOK NEWS MAILING LIST

Want to keep up with my writing schedule and get the latest book news from me? Sign up for my mailing list and read my newsletters for behind-the-scene information as well as to get free and discounted books.

Jan Thompson's Mailing List
JanThompson.com/newsletter

PLEASE WRITE A REVIEW

Thank you for reading *Love You Always*. If you'd like to leave a review, please follow the link below to see the retailers that carry this ebook.

Love You Always
JanThompson.com/love

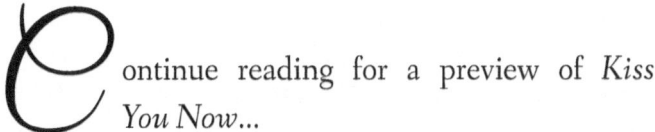ontinue reading for a preview of *Kiss You Now...*

THE NEXT BOOK IS KISS YOU NOW

SAVANNAH SWEETHEARTS BOOK 8

A novelist who can't write...
A doctor who won't practice...
A world moving on with or without them...

In Book 8 of Savannah Sweethearts, we return to
the Savannah Senior Living Resort on Tybee Island,

where centenarian Great-grandpa Hiram Jacobs waits for the day God takes him home to heaven...

HUNTER'S HONOR...

"How could he fire me? I'm his favorite great-grandson. Besides, look at all my writing awards! Yes, it's taking me a little while—okay, seven years long—to help him write his memoirs, but we're going to get it done. I promise. Great-grandpa Hiram might be losing it if he thinks a no-name people walker—what kind of a job is that?—knows more about the Jacobs family than I do."

— HUNTER JACOBS, AUTHOR IN SOME DISTRESS, REVEREND HIRAM JACOBS'S FORMER WRITING ASSISTANT

Reverend Hiram Jacobs believes he is finally dying, and he wants his memoirs published before his hundred-and-fourth birthday.

Well, Hunter has his own book deadlines to juggle, and can't Great-grandpa Hiram wait a few more months?

Unfortunately, Hunter's writing career tanks. He loses his publishing contract since his books haven't sold enough copies, and his agent fails to find a new publisher for his old manuscripts.

His writing well has dried up, and he has been unable to write anything new for months.

Hunter sells his cottage in the Swiss Alps to pay off his debts, and flies home to coastal Georgia.

He wants to talk to Great-grandpa Hiram about his memoirs, hoping that it might reboot his writing career.

To Hunter's surprise, Great-grandpa has found a new writing assistant, someone who is not in the Jacobs family.

And Hunter is required to hand over everything he has worked on for seven years to her, an outsider who barely knows Great-grandpa for a year.

Stunned, Hunter feels stuck.

PRIYANKA'S PRESENT...

"Hiram is sweet to let me write down those life stories he has been telling me when I bring flowers to the resort and walk with him in the afternoons. He thinks he's running out of time, and sadly, I agree. Before he dies, he wants to sign his hardcover memoirs for his entire family. I'm going to help him finish the book that his great-grandson is taking too many years to write. How hard can it be? It's not like emergency surgery."

— PRIYANKA PATEL, PART-TIME
PEOPLE WALKER AT THE
SAVANNAH SENIOR LIVING
RESORT, PART-TIME FLORIST AT
SEA GLASS FLOWER SHOP

Yet there's that faint scent of a defunct career, too dark, too painful for Priyanka to revisit.

Here, renting a campground yurt on Tybee Island, she is far away from the surgical centers at pediatric hospitals and from that nightmare of a medical mission trip.

These days, Priyanka would rather cheer up the elderly residents of the Savannah Senior Living Resort by bringing them freshly-cut flowers, singing and praying with them, and listening to some of them tell sad stories about their children who never come to visit anymore.

She spends mornings at the florist and afternoons at the SSLR, walking with the seniors who can, and wheeling them around if they cannot.

Hiram is Priyanka's favorite patient—ah, friend.

The centenarian is losing his memory bit by bit, and the sooner Priyanka writes down everything about his life for his posterity, the better. His great-grandson is supposed to be compiling all his sermons, and if he'd hurry up, those can be published before Hiram dies.

Still, perhaps she should have turned down Hiram's request for her to help him complete his memoirs.

And yet, her heart gets the better of her, and Priyanka says yes to helping an elderly gentleman fulfill his lifelong wish.

When life moves on and time runs out, Priyanka finds herself thrown together with Hunter, trying to catch up with the world around them that is moving faster than they can handle.

Should they press forward and go along with it, or should they shrink back and return to their comfort zones?

Or is there another way they haven't thought of?

Kiss You Now (Savannah Sweethearts Book 8):
JanThompson.com/kiss

Savannah Sweethearts:
JanThompson.com/sweethearts

For book news, sign up for Jan's mailing list:
JanThompson.com/newsletter

KISS YOU NOW CHAPTER 1
SNEAK PEEK

Fired? I'm not hearing it right.

Hunter Jacobs dragged his fingers across his two-day-old beard as he stared at the carpeted floor of his great-grandfather's bedroom, where a slice of afternoon sunlight superimposed on his polished cowboy boots he had worn all the way from his erstwhile writing chalet in Switzerland to the town where he had been born.

Sadly, he hadn't been back in Savannah in seven years.

Perhaps that had been his problem.

Then again, in the age of high-speed internet and ubiquitous Wi-Fi, it didn't matter how far apart he was from his great-grandfather.

Right?

Hunter breathed in deeply. The room smelled of...

Lavender?

Hunter lifted his eyes toward Great-grandpa Hiram Jacobs, lying down on his hospital bed in the center of the room, his feet in socks crossed at the ankles, his arms folded across his chest, and his eyes closed.

There were many years of lines on Great-grandpa's face, and his bushy eyebrows reminded Hunter of his own grandfather, who had passed away a couple of decades ago when Hunter had been in middle school.

Great-grandpa had outlived most of his children, save for a daughter in a nursing home somewhere. For some reason—genetic, perhaps—the centenarian patriarch of the Jacobs family was still going strong. A reverend who had retired too many times, he was now back preaching the Sunday morning services at this Savannah Senior Living Resort.

I'm sure he has much to preach about.

Hence, the problem.

With so many years of history to collect, Hunter wasn't sure Great-grandpa was ready to write his memoirs.

Memoir, perhaps, but memoirs?

Hunter chuckled. "Great-grandpa, I didn't hear you right. I thought you said *fired*. Did you mean hired? As in I'm still hired?"

Great-grandpa opened his eyes.

They were blue, like Hunter's father's eyes. His own were brown. He had taken after his mother. Brown hair, brown eyes, the works.

Some years ago, Hunter thought he might grow a foot. Well, it hadn't happened. He would be forever be stuck at five feet and ten inches, while all his cousins towered over six feet tall.

He rocked on the ball of his cowboy boots, his favorite because its stacked heel added almost two inches to his height. Finally, he'd be at the same height as his teenage cousins.

The sound of a sharp sound drew his attention back to Great-grandpa, who snapped his fingers again.

Hunter wasn't sure what had happened.

His mind had bounced from memoirs to cowboy boots.

"I'm a bit jet-lagged," Hunter said. "Maybe we can talk about this tomorrow? I drove here straight from the airport, and my suitcases are still in the trunk."

Great-grandpa frowned. "I said *fired*."

Uh-oh.

So he did say I'm fired.

Story of my life.

Hunter felt he had to sit down, but there was nowhere to sit. The only armchair in the room was filled with a pile of folded laundry.

"I hired you seven years ago," Great-grandpa continued. "Where's my manuscript?"

"A hundred years are a lot to compile," Hunter tried to explain.

"A hundred and three, almost four. Not your worry anymore. I have a new writing assistant now. She can type a mile a minute. She'll get my memoirs done before our family reunion."

"She? She who?" *Please don't let it be Aunt Delilah.*

Great-grandpa's youngest granddaughter, Aunt Delilah had fancied herself as the scribe of the family, but she spun tales like a spider spun webs. "To spice it up," she'd say, embellishing everything.

"Who, Great-grandpa?" Hunter asked again, in case he hadn't heard him.

"My next birthday is coming up." Great-grandpa seemed to have moved on to a more important topic.

"Your birthday isn't until the end of June. It's only February."

Then again, Mom had talked about that over the phone many times for the last six months. She would call Hunter to remind him to buy this and that from Switzerland and other parts of Europe that Hunter hadn't had time for.

Alas, his time in Switzerland was over. He had sold his chalet to pay off his debts—or more accurately, to return the advance his publisher had given him.

The family reunion would be in about two months, though Hunter's initial plan had been to skip the party. He had several late book deadlines and writer's blocks—yes, plural—and so much work to do he didn't know where to begin.

All that was moot now. His publisher had told him to take a hike, but first, they wanted his advance back.

His agent had suggested self-publishing.

Indie publishing.

That was the new terminology for such a thing.

Hunter wondered if anyone wanted to read his

Arthurian medieval high fantasy tale of a down-and-out knight, set in a near-future dystopian alternate universe he had yet to name. No, he had edited out the space program. His revised plot was very down-to-earth. Seriously.

"Are you coming to my birthday party?" Great-grandpa's voice slapped his cheeks.

Hunter stared at the mass of wrinkles on the old preacher's face.

"You mean the family reunion? That's the one in two months."

"I'm sure they'll throw me a surprise birthday along with it. Happens every year."

Hunter chuckled. "And you just acted surprised?"

"Every single time. Are you going to be there?"

"I'm in town, but I could be working."

Great-grandpa was probably not aware that Hunter had lost his job, his money, his house. So, yeah, he needed a job.

"I hope it's not too surprising," Great-grandpa carried on. "The last time we threw a surprise birthday party for your aunt Moira, she dropped dead at the door from a heart attack."

I could use that in my book.

Yeah, the one that could never be published.

"That was at least six or seven years ago," Hunter said, somehow aware of his entire family tree looking down at him and wagging branches at him that seemed to say, "You should come home more often."

"Did you write it down?"

"Write what down?" *All my failures?*

"Moira's funeral. I want that in my memoir."

"Your memoir is now ten volumes long, Great-grandpa." One volume for every epic decade he had lived.

Actually, they would have to add an eleventh volume if Great-grandpa kept on living.

How could anyone live so long?

Hunter had wondered if Great-grandpa's birth certificate had been wrong. Nope. This wonderful man of God had truly been born at the end of World War I.

Seriously.

So much to tell.

So little time.

"Get Moira in my book."

"Yes, sir—uh, Great-grandpa."

Funny how Great-grandpa had insisted that the young ones called him by his full title, always emphasizing *great*. To be sure, Great-grandpa was a humble man—except for that. He'd rather they not call him *sir*, because he hadn't been knighted.

Knights?

Like those in my Arthurian—

What am I thinking about?

It's over.

My career. My goals. My livelihood.

Over.

Hunter tried to blot out any memories of his failed attempt at keeping a career. All those best-selling lists meant nothing to him now if he couldn't pay his rent and had to go home to Mom's basement.

Unfortunately, if he went to Mom's house in Nashville, she was sure to ask him about his books. When would that Arthurian whatever be published?

Now it might never be.

"Good. Turn over everything you've written down to my new memoirist." Great-grandpa tried to sit up.

As Hunter helped him, he smelled lavender on his collar.

Soap?

"Does she have a name?" Hunter asked.

"She? How did you know she's a she?"

"You said earlier, 'She can type a mile a minute.' I heard you."

"Glad you were paying attention." Great-grandpa patted Hunter's hand. "Good boy."

"You didn't answer my question." Hunter reminded himself that he had to remain calm.

"What question?"

"Her name?"

"Whose name?"

"Your writing assistant."

Great-grandpa waved his arm. "Oh, you don't know her."

"Yikes. She's not even family?" *Whew. It's not Aunt Delilah, after all.*

"And you're family?" Great-grandpa stared at Hunter.

"Yeah."

"When was the last time you came to see me?"

"Ah... But we have FaceTime. Email."

"Seven years ago," Great-grandpa reminded him. "At my brother Phil's funeral."

"I had to work."

Great-grandpa pointed a knobby finger at Hunter. "Work is more important to you than family."

"No."

"Walk the talk then."

Hunter could feel a small sermon coming, flying at his face.

He didn't need the reminder that he had to get right with God. Work had kept him so busy that his church attendance had now been down to listening to online sermons broadcasted from Riverside Chapel in Savannah. He considered that to be his home church.

He knew what Great-grandpa was going to say next.

Online churches cannot replace real-time face-to-face church attendance.

But if Great-grandpa only knew how busy he had been...

Too busy for church.

Too busy for family.

"If you worship work, then work is your idol," Great-grandpa said.

"I don't worship work!"

"What does Matthew 6:33 say?" the preacher asked.

Bible quiz. I better not fail this one.

But Hunter couldn't remember the verse.

"Seek..."

Great-grandpa waited.

"Ah..." Hunter cleared his throat. "Seek..."

Search? Find? Hunt?

Something...

Silence in the room.

Then Hunter heard a melodious voice, tinged with a soft and light accent from somewhere he couldn't place right away.

"It says, 'But seek first the kingdom of God and His righteousness, and all these things shall be added to you.' Matthew 6:33."

Cascading brown hair shimmering over tanned

shoulders glided past Hunter. "Hello, Pastor Hiram."

She didn't even look at Hunter.

In her hands was a bouquet of fresh lavender.

~

Kiss You Now (Savannah Sweethearts 8):
JanThompson.com/kiss

More Information about Savannah Sweethearts:
JanThompson.com/savannah

To keep up with Jan Thompson's book news:
JanThompson.com/newsletter

ACKNOWLEDGMENTS

I write these Savannah Sweethearts stories of sweet, clean, wholesome, and inspirational Christian romances to uplift and encourage my readers on both good and bad days in life. This particular story about Camden and Iris is a reminder that "God walks with us through both expected and unexpected difficult times on earth," as Pastor Flores said in this novel.

For law enforcement and police procedural fact checking, I thank Detective Dony Jay, SWAT Deputy Joshua Hood, and private investigator and former FBI agent Steven Kerry Brown.

For postmortem fact checking, I thank Dr. Judy Melinek, forensic pathologist and coauthor with T. J. Mitchell of *Working Stiff: Two Years, 262 Bodies, and the Making of a Medical Examiner*, for her expertise.

For real estate information, I thank my husband, who is a Realtor and an information technology consultant. It's nice to have a resident expert.

As per usual, not all of my extensive research

materials make it into my books, but I feel that it is necessary to thank everyone for their time and kindness in answering my many questions.

And yes, any mistake is mine.

Many thanks to my Georgia Press publishing team for keeping up with my writing schedule.

For this novel, I thank my outstanding copyeditor, Dori Harrell, and my patient proofreader, Lenda Selph. Their eyes for details are from the Lord.

I am grateful to God for my husband and son for their support and encouragement. I also thank God for my parents and my three brothers for my happy and memorable childhood. I'll always remember my beloved mother and my late father for having instilled in me the love of reading and writing from a very early age. I miss my father here on earth, but I will see him again in heaven someday.

Most of all, I am eternally thankful to my Lord and Savior, Jesus Christ, who died on the cross to save me from my sins and rose again from the grave to give me eternal life. Without Him, I can write nothing (John 15:5).

Jan Thompson
John 3:16

ABOUT JAN THOMPSON

USA Today bestselling author Jan Thompson writes clean and wholesome contemporary Christian romance with elements of women's fiction, Christian romantic suspense with an air of mystery, and inspirational international thrillers with threads of sweet Christian romance. Jan's books are for readers who love inspiring stories of faith, hope, and love in Jesus Christ.

Raised on a tropical island in the eastern hemisphere, Jan now lives and writes in the western hemisphere. Her international background gives her a unique multicultural and multiracial perspective to her novels and books. The island has never left her, and she reminisces about beach life in her beach romance novels.

When Jan is not busy writing small-town stories, she writes big-city romantic suspense and international technothrillers, a nod to her previous career in computer science. She weaves technology with human interests, reflecting the current and future digital world. And romance. There's always romance.

Beyond the printed page, Jan is a wife, mother, family scribe, avid reader, occasional artist, erstwhile pianist, and chief of staff to the family cat.

❧

Find out more about Jan Thompson:
JanThompson.com

Subscribe to Jan's book news mailing list:
JanThompson.com/newsletter

For God so loved the world
that He gave His only begotten Son,
that whoever believes in Him
should not perish
but have everlasting life.
—John 3:16